BRAVE

WEST

WIND

BRAVE
WEST
WIND

Captain Buddy Ward

QP BOOKS
New Orleans, Louisiana

BRAVE WEST WIND

a novel

Published in 2016 by QP Books, an imprint of Quid Pro Books.

QUID PRO, LLC
5860 Citrus Blvd., Suite D-101
New Orleans, Louisiana 70123
www.qpbooks.com

ISBN 978-1-61027-342-8 (paperback)
ISBN 978-1-61027-345-9 (hardcover)
ISBN 978-1-61027-343-5 (eBook)

This is a work of fiction. Names, characters, incidents, locales, and characterizations either are a product of the author's imagination or are used fictitiously. Any resemblance to actual names, persons (living or dead), places, or events is entirely coincidental.

Publisher's Cataloging-in-Publication

Ward, Captain Buddy.
    Brave West Wind / Captain Buddy Ward.
      p. cm.
    ISBN 978-1-61027-342-8 (pbk.)

1. Ship captains—Fiction. 2. Key West (Fla.)—Fiction. 3. Kidnapping—Fiction. I. Title.
PR9199.4.W33 2016   813.'1'3871—dc22
                                        2016536735
                                               CIP

TO MY WIFE LEE ANNE,
THE LOVE OF ALL MY LIFETIMES

WHO HELD MY HAND AS WE JUMPED FROM THE CLIFF
AND LIVED THE GRAND ADVENTURE.

IT WAS HER SPARK THAT BREATHED
LIFE INTO THIS STORY.

BRAVE WEST WIND

PROLOGUE

The hot sticky surface of the sea was mirror smooth. Not a ripple in sight, nothing to hint at the oncoming storm. Nothing except the high dark clouds gathering on the southwestern horizon. Suddenly a slight gust of wind hurried across the surface leaving a distinctive trail as it passed. Another gust arrived heralding the approach of the storm. The surface was somehow changed. It was no longer smooth, but began to have more of the effect of velvet. There was another puff, and again another until the breath of the gods became constant and unyielding. The swells arrived marching in straight lines from the Southwest. They were small at first but strong and deep and spoke to what was coming.

The rain began, thick and gloppy. The sounds of the rain disguised the wind which was now howling. The wind and the rain increased in coverage and intensity, blowing the surface of the sea up the face of the ever-intensifying swells, churning the water into a thick white froth. The cold fresh rain poured down upon the tropical sea. The smell of the storm was suddenly apparent. The wind drove the needle-like raindrops horizontally into the building swells that now topped twenty feet. The air here above the surface was now totally consumed with the storm. The deafening roar of wind and rain mixed with the crashing waves.

Imperceptibly, the swell direction changed. Somewhere to the west an eye had formed with blue skies and calm winds, but not here, where the storm raged and consumed everything in its path. Nothing could stand against its unstoppable power and uncontrolled violence. The storm roared as it reached its apex. The unending swells stacked one upon the other, each one bigger than the last.

Then it was done. It took several hours for the wind and rain to subside, hours more for the swells to die down. By late afternoon gossamer ribbons of sunlight peeked through the menacing clouds. All about, the storm had left its mark. The frothy surface and the murky rainwater had turned the surface into an indistinguishable landscape. All had been changed by the storm, which now moved on to a more fertile environment.

It was that time of morning, not quite light, no longer dark. The sleek, shiny fiberglass hull of the sloop rode at anchor in harmony with the forces of nature. Ripples of gentle wavelets lapped along the sides of *Zonda*. The anchor line stretched over the bow pulpit and reached down into the shimmering clear waters of the Great Bahamas banks. The heavy plow-shaped anchor dug in, holding fast to the white sand bottom.

Almost undetectable at first, the sounds began to change. The rhythm of the sea became unsettled as the plastic paddles made their way through the quiet water. There were muffled squeaks and groans, as the rubber dinghy rubbed alongside the sailboat's hull. Time passed in undisturbed silence. Suddenly there were four distinct noises: two muffled thuds, followed by scuffling, then another thump as a large bundle was lowered down into the small, inflatable boat followed by the two men. They no longer felt the need for silence; a quick pull and the outboard sputtered, then sprang to life.

The small, high-speed propeller whipped the salty brine into lines of white foam, and an eerie phosphine glow traced the path of the rubber raft as it raced south toward the island of Andros.

The sky began to glow with a soft red hue toward the east. A brilliant white light appeared below deck. Instantaneously, the light filled the cabin, then spewed forth from every opening. The deafening crack of the explosion preceded the appearance of the flames. In seconds, the searing white light was transformed into a large golden fireball that engulfed the helpless yacht. The stately aluminum mast began to twist and melt in the intense heat. The gnarled metal spar crashed across the blackened remains of *Zonda* and fell into the pristine waters with a loud hiss. The sun rose and illuminated the scene of total and instantaneous annihilation that lay beneath clouds of thick black smoke.

1

Captain Steamer Causey lay on the whistle as he took *War Eagle* through the last turn of the narrow channel near Shark Reef Cay. He reached for the throttles and gently slid them forward. There was a slight change in the sound of the engines as the turbocharger engaged. The Caterpillars would push her along at better than thirty knots, but Steamer rarely ran her that fast.

Rybovich Boat Yard had built many beautiful yachts, but none more so than *War Eagle*. The hull was midnight black with a thin gold stripe for accent. The cap-rail was all mahogany. Each piece of the rich wood had been spliced and laminated so that it conformed perfectly to her shape. The transom, too, was all mahogany with both an image of an eagle and the boat's name painted in gold. Above the wooden cap-rail, she was all white. The fishing cockpit was decked in well-oiled teak wood. There was a large, complex fighting chair made of stainless steel, mahogany, and vinyl as well as a well-stocked bait-rigging station and a built in refrigerated fish-box.

Mr. Bailey owned *War Eagle* but the flying bridge belonged to Steamer. He had diligently overseen the selection and the installation of the instruments and electronics. In Steamer's eyes, she was the finest fishing machine ever built, and he cared for her as if she were his own.

The sharp, pointed bow of her sleek black hull rose up as if to sniff the morning air. With his powerful right arm, Steamer swung the helm hard over and turned southeast. *War Eagle* and her sixty-five feet of fishing luxury began the hunt.

Jimmy Morgan climbed the ladder to the flying bridge and handed the captain a cup of coffee. "Steamer," the young Bahamian said in the lyrical dialect of the Caribbean, "why do you always use the whistle when you leave? Do you think anyone is crazy enough to get in front of you?"

"No, Jimmy, I do it because when I do, you bring me coffee." When Steamer spoke, his voice sounded like a growl. He wore a uniform consisting of black cotton pants and a black twill shirt with a *War Eagle* logo. His attire seemed to complement his muscle tone and development.

"Oh, now, so the great Captain Steamer thinks his own personal galley slave must answer to whistles."

"Thank you for the coffee, Jimmy. Is that better?" Steamer said curtly as he set the autopilot, turned the helm seat sideways, and propped his long legs up onto the console. "How are they doing down there?"

"They aren't gonna make it. They all got into the rum last night. The one named Jenkins—he already heaved."

"Make sure you take care of the one named Maxwell. Mr. Bailey says he's a special customer, and he wants him to catch a fish."

"I will see to it, Steamer. Mr. Maxwell will catch a very large fish—a tuna or a marlin. He will have a very good time. Then he will take care of Jimmy?" The small-framed man had short-cropped hair and a round face that gave him a boyish appearance when he smiled.

"I'm sure he will, but if he doesn't, let me know. I know Mr. Bailey will help out; he's been very good to me."

"Okay, Steamer, I'll take your word. Just don't forget who does all the work while you sit up here like a king."

"Tell me, Jimmy, who's doing the work now? Shouldn't you be rigging baits?" The two men continued to banter as *War Eagle* charged seaward.

The clear water took on a bluish haze, then in spectacular fashion turned a brilliant shade of dark blue as they crossed the ledge into deep water.

"Well, here we are," said Jimmy as he returned to the cockpit. "Mr. Maxwell, why don't you go first?"

Danny Maxwell was larger than the other anglers by at least sixty pounds. He was in his mid-fifties and was deceptively quick for a big man.

"Where're we at, boy?" Maxwell said in a deep Louisiana drawl as he lit a cigar.

"We are at 'Tongue of the Ocean,' Mr. Maxwell, a place you will remember all your life," Jimmy said, without flinching. "It is where the big fish live, the tuna and the marlin." The young Bahamian escorted the angler to the chair, and then began rigging baits.

Steamer eased the throttles back to trolling speed, and Jimmy streamed five baits and a teaser in the turbulent water astern. "Would anyone like something to drink?" Jimmy asked.

Maxwell removed his cigar long enough to order a beer. "And not any of that Bahamian shit. I want a Bud."

"And how about you, Mr. Jenkins?"

"No, thank you," Steve Jenkins mumbled weakly. He sat on the deck with his back braced against the bulkhead. A slight burp warned him that he could no longer contain the contents of his stomach. In a clumsy, violent action, he suddenly bolted for the rail and heaved over the side. Jimmy disappeared into the cabin and returned with two beers, a towel, and a large white bucket. He handed the Budweiser to Mr. Maxwell, then went to the aid of Mr. Jenkins.

"Here, Mr. Jenkins, an ice cold Kalik, finest beer in all of the islands. It will chase away the demons of the rum." Jimmy was in the process of washing down the area where the angler had heaved when he saw the long column of smoke in the sky towards the north. "I will be right back," he announced, and then climbed to the bridge.

Steamer scanned the electronic arrays that lay before him and glanced about the boundless ocean that surrounded him, then turned his attention to the ritual of sharpening the knife that was his prized possession. In many ways it was his only possession. When the rum began to cloud his mind and ease his tongue, Steamer was often heard to say, "The weak squander away their precious life force trying to protect trinkets and baubles. The only treasures in life are those things that sustain it." The knife was his sole exception. He carried it always, cradled in a supple black leather sheath slung low on his hip in the manner of an Old West gunslinger. The tempered blade, razor-sharp, gleamed in the sunlight as it swirled about in the small pool of fine oil. Then came a high-pitched rasp as the steel edge resisted the porous stone. The deer-horn handle was always polished to a mirror finish.

The knife had become the embodiment of all that he was capable of when he reached down into his center. Second Lieutenant Thomas W. Causey had received it the day he graduated from Ranger training at Fort Benning. During his survival training in the swamps and forests near Egland, Florida, in an unusual display of luck and skill, Steamer had found himself hidden in a tree with a spear he had made by tying a knife into a split bamboo pole with part of his shoestring.

Reminiscing, Steamer looked up into the cloudless sky, closed his eyes, and saw it once again: the large buck had stepped delicately from the clearing and stopped beneath the tree. The fine tan hairs of its velvet hide had bristled in the light breeze. "Easy … easy now." Steamer sat motionless concentrating on controlling his every breath. He had been so close that he could smell the animal. Without warning the great buck began to rub and scrape his antlers along the trunk of the tree, gouging and tearing the bark. On a particularly violent scrape, the deer momentarily hung a point of its rack, exposing its neck to Steamer's spear. That action was its final mistake. Within the hour, Steamer had butchered the carcass, cleaned the area, and stored the meat in a nearby stream. What had once been a three-day exercise in survival would now feed his team for a week. The legend followed him, and his comrades celebrated the feat by having a knife handle made from one of the horns.

"Steamer! Captain Steamer, look, over there!" Steamer was startled when Jimmy appeared on the bridge. "What is it?" Jimmy asked as he pointed to the column of smoke.

"I have no idea, Jimmy," he said as he lowered his binoculars.

"I think we should go over there." Jimmy was earnestly concerned.

"Keep your voice down," Steamer chastised. "Have you lost your mind? That's at least twenty miles away, and it's someone else's problem. If you think I'm gonna mess up this charter and go traipsing off chasin' my tail, then you've been smokin' too much of that loco weed."

"But, Steamer, we must do something!"

"You get back down there and tend to the customers. I'll get in touch with BASRA."

"Fish on!" came the cry from the cockpit.

"Well, they're home," yelled Steamer as he disengaged the autopilot and brought the engines to dead slow. Jimmy slid down the ladder and took control of the cockpit.

"Easy now, Mr. Maxwell. Let him chew the tasty fish. We want him to take the hook all the way to his belly." For a second time, the large billfish thrashed his way into the baits. Seconds passed. Two of the baits tangled and began to strip line from the reels.

"These aren't the ones you want," Jimmy coaxed the big fish as he took his knife and freed the tangled lines. "This one." He said quietly as he eased himself toward the starboard side outrigger. "This succulent, tender fish over here that Jimmy has prepared for you."

The warm shimmering water flowed across its silvery gill plates as the great blue marlin once again changed course and re-crossed the boat's wake. The baitfish that had been so recently savaged began to quickly disappear behind him in the shadowy sea. The fish hesitated for an instant. It was not too late to turn and seize the wounded prey. From the corner of his mammoth eye, the marlin saw a fresh bait skipping just below the surface a mere ten feet away. Ancient feeding instincts took control of the giant and with a decisive stroke of his mighty tail, the fish crashed into the shiny blue runner rigged with a blue and white skirt and a ten-aught hook. The giant marlin swallowed and dove for the bottom.

The large Fin-Nor reel began to sing as the line stripped out at an ever-accelerating pace. "Get ready now, Mr. Maxwell," Jimmy said as he lifted the rod from its holder and moved toward the man in the chair. *"Set!"* he yelled, and Steamer drove the throttles to full. With all his strength, Jimmy strained against the weight of the fish as the hook set deep into its flesh. Seconds later Jimmy handed the rod to Danny Maxwell, and Steamer eased the engines back to dead slow. The long, arduous battle had begun.

Steamer sat back and once again turned his attention to the long column of smoke rising into the morning sky some distance to the west. "Shark Reef Cay, Shark Reef Cay, come back," he said into the microphone of the VHF radio. For several moments he waited in silence. "Shark Reef Cay, Shark Reef Cay, come back," he repeated.

"This is Jane at the store. Can I help you?" Jane Carter was an elegant woman who lived on Nassau but worked in the only store on Shark Reef Cay three days a week.

"Jane, this is *War Eagle*. I need for you to make a call for me if you can."

"Certainly, Captain Steamer."

"Would you call Mr. Murray, the customs officer, for me, and ask him to call me on the radio?"

"Certainly, I will call him right away. The store is clear with *War Eagle*."

Blue turned to black as the marlin dove for the safety of the abyss. There was not yet a sense of panic in the movements of the giant. He had felt the hook before and had found freedom awaiting him in the depths of the sea.

Twenty minutes passed. The great fish continued to sound. The marlin was now diving for his life, pushing for the limits of his own endurance, testing the mettle of the equipment and the resolve of the man who had engaged him.

The big man sweated profusely, and his breathing became labored and shallow. Jimmy saw to the man's needs as the angler battled the giant fish beneath the now blazing tropical sun. The third and final knot appeared as the line ran from the spool and disappeared beneath the surface. "Three hundred yards left, Captain!" Jimmy called out, then took a wet rag and began wiping Maxwell's face.

In the silence and the darkness of the deep ocean the tide of battle ebbed. The great fish had begun to tire. Alone in the darkness he sensed danger. The grey shadows were gathering, circling just beyond the reaches of his senses. If freedom did not come soon, he would have to return the fight to the surface.

Jimmy noticed a slight aspect change in the line as the billfish leveled off and changed direction. "Steamer, he's coming up! Go right! Go right!" Maxwell groaned as he began to pump the reel, regaining line at a painstakingly slow rate. "Here he comes, Steamer; I see him now!" Jimmy was leaning over the transom as the great fish raced towards him. In a furious display of power and grace, the marlin broke the surface for the first time.

"This is the customs office calling *War Eagle*." John Murray's voice filled the air.

"Mr. Murray, this is Steamer Causey on the *War Eagle*. There is a large column of smoke somewhere near Northwest Channel Light. I was wondering if you would be able to call Bahamian Air Sea Rescue and ask them to check it out."

"That would be no problem, Captain Steamer. I will call them right away. Will you be responding also?"

"I think not, Mr. Murray. I'm all the way down to Tongue of the Ocean, and I have a charter on board. It would be quicker for BASRA to check it out from the air."

"I will pass that on, Captain. By the way, how is the fishing?"

"We are just about to wire our first of the day. Looks like a blue somewhere around 250."

"Very nice," John Murray responded. "I will call BASRA right away and I'll call you back with what they find. Good luck to you. This is the customs office clear."

"No need, Mr. Murray; we'll be returning to Shark Reef Cay tonight. I'll see you then. *War Eagle* clear."

The fish made a final lunge but was stopped short as it slammed broadside into the painted surface of the black hull. The braided line once again filled the reel. The black snap swivel and six feet of the leader wire were all now above the water. Steamer stopped the engines and went below to help Jimmy with the gaffing of the fish.

"A prize, Captain," Jimmy said softly, "a truly wonderful fish." With all their strength, captain and crew hauled the blue marlin aboard. "There, Mr. Maxwell, I told you this was a special place. Let me congratulate you on the outstanding job you did in landing this trophy fish."

"Thanks, boy. How 'bout bring me a beer when ya finish with the fish. I'll be in the cabin coolin' off."

2

There were six in all, two men and four women, taking refuge from the heat of the afternoon sun. They sat beneath a grove of young palm trees that provided the only shade available at the Shark Reef Cay Club Marina. They sat and sewed, mending the worn and frayed pieces of an old mainsail. The sail had the look of ancient yellowed parchment, but when the mariners entwined their skills, the fabric became far more supple and resilient than it first appeared.

Without looking up from his work, a thin, bearded man asked, "Where are you bound?" He spoke in soft, gentle tones void of any accent which may have offered clues to his past.

"Panama, eventually," the answer came from an older woman whose short, cropped hair accentuated her solid frame.

Colin Sinclair, a tall man with thick, snow-white hair stood up, slid the pipe from between his teeth, and turned to address the group. "We understand it's a wonderful place to retire. The cost of living is minimal, the climate is pleasant, and the sailing is fabulous."

As he approached his mate of thirty years, Polly reached for him.

"It all sounds so grand, doesn't it, Colin?" she said softly as they joined hands. Polly turned her attention back to the group and, without releasing her lover's hand, continued, "But we must take one detour first."

Colin once again removed his pipe and took a deep breath. "We've got to go back to the States for a while. There is a great deal of paperwork involved with Social Security and travel visas and such."

"And the children. We're going to spend some time with the children and the grandchildren. As it stands now, we'll be leaving for Fort Lauderdale sometime tomorrow." Polly stood and wrapped her arms about her man.

"Best leave early," the thin, bearded man warned. "It's over eighty miles to Gun Cay."

"It doesn't matter," Colin said as he held his mate. "It'll take *Fidelity* two days at least. She's like us, getting on in years and not liking to be rushed."

"We'll get as far as we can," Polly responded, "then anchor out somewhere on the banks."

"A small island of humanity nestled in the limitless sea."

"Colin, that's so poetic," Polly said. "You must write that into the log." She turned her attention back to the group and back to the task at hand.

3

"Charlie, Charlie, come back!" A cloud of dust assaulted the peaceful group of sailors as Marvin Proctor rushed by in the old abused golf cart. This was not an act of malice: Marvin was simply rushing to begin the preparations for the return of the fishing fleet.

A piece of rusted metal fell from beneath the cart as the front wheels bumped across a timber used to protect an electrical connection. Marvin sped around the corner of the steel building that served as a maintenance shop for the marina.

"Charlimon, don't you hear me calling you on the radio?"

Charlie Baxter burned a long drag of his joint, closed his eyes, and held his breath as the marijuana took hold and eased his mind and body. "What chu worrin' me for? I told you dis mornin', the radio's broken."

"It's not broken, Charlimon. You just got to turn the damn thing on. What am I gonna do with you? You know, if Mr. Webster comes and finds you here all high on ganja, he'll fire us both. I can't have that, Charlie. You know I have a wife and a child on Nassau. I need this job."

Smoke poured from Charlie's nose and mouth, as his laugh became a cough. He leaned to one side and spit on the ground. "Now that's a fine one, you with a wife and child. Who you think you talkin' to, mon? I been wit chu on every island for three hundred miles. How many wives and children you got now?" He pushed the dreadlocks up from his face and once again brought the hand-rolled cigarette to his mouth.

Instead of the peace and serenity of the intoxicating fumes, waves of pain and nausea rushed in upon Charlie. Marvin's attack had been swift, decisive, and unexpected. Charlie sat motionless with his head pinned to the corrugated aluminum wall. He gasped for air as he felt Marvin's fingers encircle his windpipe. He was overcome by the smell of his assailant's breath as Marvin whispered just inches away from his ear.

"I'm not playing wit chu, Charlimon. I want you back to work right away, and if Mr. Webster asks me anything about chu, I will fire you on the spot." As Marvin released his grip, Charlie lost his balance and fell to the side. Marvin reached down for a large plastic freezer bag half filled with the dried remains of the contraband. "Were did you get this? There is nothing here but twigs and seeds."

"Free sample, Mo," Charlie said as he regained his composure and snatched the bag from Marvin's grasp.

"There were some crazy commandos passing it out like candy and asking questions."

"Here?"

"No, down on Andros."

"When were you on Andros?"

"Last night after you left the bar."

"And who did you find crazy enough to take you to Andros?"

"Oh, nobody, mon, nobody would take us." Charlie began to ease away from Marvin preparing for his needed escape. "Das why we had to borrow a boat."

"Whose boat, Charlimon?"

"Yours." The damage done, Charlie leaped across a rusted old engine block and raced down the dock with Marvin Proctor in close pursuit. Charlie was still running at full speed when he dove from the end of the dock into the crystalline water. He looked around him in an effort to extend the peaceful solitude. Small colorful striped fish darted about seeking shelter beneath the dock. A group of live conchs lay on the bottom tied together by a string, awaiting their call to the dinner table. An urgency began to swell within him, and his need for air inevitably drove him to the surface. A large rusted bolt made a whistling sound as Marvin hurled it at Charlie's head.

"I was hopin' for a shark, but even the fish got better things to do than play wit chu. It's almost time. While you are in the water, make yourself useful and get some conch."

"They are only three down here," he lied.

"Then you must get some more," Marvin said as he walked back towards the cart.

"Can I use your boat?"

"No! Swim!" Marvin said without looking up. Charlie waited until Marvin was out of sight, then swam over to Marvin's boat and climbed in.

The loose stones provided little traction, and Marvin was in a hurry. The tires spun momentarily as the rusted cart sped around the corner of the building. He glanced at his watch, then raced toward the weigh station.

The air began to resonate with a low drone, barely audible at first. The sound seemed to come from somewhere beyond the new houses that had been built along the high bluff. The inhabitants of the marina stood silently staring seaward as awareness of the sound spread across the tiny island like the shadow of a cloud moving across the ground on a brisk spring day. The decibel level increased. Marvin and his team of five locals stood at the weigh station. They were all dressed in white knit shirts with the Shark Reef Cay Club embroidered over the pocket.

The sound soon became a roar akin to that of a buffalo stampede or a dozen whirlwinds descending on the once quiet village. The first of the noisy intruders to enter the channel was the sleek black hull of *War Eagle*. Steamer jerked the throttles back and the responsive yacht stepped down from her plane and squatted into her following wake. This was admittedly a showy entrance that was not entirely safe. But Steamer had always had a flair for the dramatic and could not resist the opportunity to display *War Eagle*'s grace and agility. Besides, it was always good for business to be the first in line especially when you had fish to weigh.

Steamer was now one with the boat as he guided the sleek black beauty effortlessly through the marina.

"Excuse me, sirs. Stand aside please, stand aside." Jimmy emerged from the salon wearing a clean uniform. The black twill shirt and white shorts had been pressed and heavily starched. He called them his picture clothes. Jimmy had always been fastidious about his dress and grooming. He took great pride in his position aboard the finest charter fishing boat in the islands. "Captain Steamer and I will have you safely ashore in just a few moments." Jimmy opened a storage locker on the port side and removed four black and gold mooring lines. As Steamer pivoted the majestic yacht just inches away from the corner pilings, Jimmy scampered about readying lines and setting fenders.

"Welcome, welcome back to Shark Reef Cay," Marvin said as he took the lines from Jimmy and made them fast to the pier. "I hope that you were successful? It was such a fine day."

"Mr. Maxwell has a large marlin and a fine wahoo to weigh," Jimmy announced proudly as he lifted the lid of the fish box. A crowd was beginning to gather. "And Mr. Jenkins has three dolphin fish that he has donated to the kitchen for this evening's meal." Marvin and one of his men came aboard and began helping Jimmy unload the fish. Steamer was making an entry in his log when he was suddenly aware of the big man standing behind him.

"Capt'n, wonder if we could talk a spell." Steamer spun around in the helm seat and motioned for Maxwell to sit down. "Naw, won't take long. Bailey tells me you've been with 'im quite a spell, eh?"

"Seven years, maybe eight. Mr. Bailey has always been a good man to work for."

"He tells me you really know your way round down here. Says ya pretty good in a tight spot, too."

"I get by," Steamer said quietly. He didn't like the direction the conversation was going but did not want to anger Mr. Bailey's friend.

"I've been down here watching a situation that appears to have gone brown on me. There were some badass revolutionaries trying to buy some guns. We know they were here but they never showed at the drop site. I'd kinda like you to keep your eyes and ears open and report back to me. In fact, the Company does some business down here from time to time and we often need a boat driver who can handle delicate situations. I think we can use you, son, but not on this flashy piece-a-shit...."

Steamer jumped to his feet.

"Whoa, boy!" Maxwell said as he met Steamer's eye. "Nothin' personal, son. I just mean it's too high profile. Ya know what I mean? We do things a little quieter."

Steamer hated Maxwell's implications. He wanted nothing more to do with the American government, covert or otherwise. "Mr. Maxwell, I don't know what you want, but I know I'm not your man. I'm a fishing boat captain. I came to the islands for the peace and quiet. I like it down here. I don't bother anyone and no one bothers me. I enjoy working for Mr. Bailey, and I intend to keep things just as they are. Now if you will excuse me, I need to start cleaning up."

Maxwell stared coldly into Steamer's eyes, then slowly turned and descended the ladder. As he stepped from the boat, he turned back to Steamer. "I wish ya luck on that. Keeping things the way they are, I mean. Sometimes it's just not that easy." Maxwell stepped onto the dock and began walking towards his room. Steve Jenkins had hit the ground running and was already in the bar nursing a cold beer and promising anyone who'd listen that he was never going to sea again.

Jimmy had prepared the chalkboard and was standing beside the trophy fish. He was holding a sign that read:

283 lb Blue Marlin, Angler: Mr. Maxwell, caught aboard War Eagle, Shark Reef Cay, Bahamas. "Over here, Mr. Maxwell, we are waiting for you to have your picture taken with this fine fish."

"Come 'er', boy. I need to talk at cha." Jimmy obediently stepped toward Maxwell who was gathering his belongings. "I ain't much on pictures," the big man said as he reached into his pocket. "How bout doin' something with the fish? Will you do that for me, boy?" Maxwell handed Jimmy two hundred dollars, slapped him on the back, and walked off.

"Yes, sir," Jimmy said quietly. He sent the marlin to the freezer in the kitchen and slowly walked back to the boat. "Mr. Maxwell is an asshole."

"What's the matter, Jimmy? He stiff you?" Steamer asked as he handed his mate a cold Kalik.

"No, he done me fine. But the fish, he deserve better than dat, you know. It was a fine fish and he deserved better."

"We all do, my friend. We all do," Steamer said as he raised his bottle as a toast, then leaned back into the fighting chair and closed his eyes.

4

The intensity of the sun began to wane, still a full hour before lesser men would notice. But Steamer knew that the time of sunset had arrived. He stepped out of the salon and looked around. Now shed of the white heat of the tropical day, the sky seemed richer, filled with soft, glowing hues of reds and violets. Jimmy was overseeing as Marvin's work crew completed the last of their cleaning tasks.

"How'd they do, Jimmy?"

"They did a fine job, sir. But you gotta stay behind 'em all the time."

"Marvin, you and your boys thirsty? There's some left over Kalik in the cooler."

"Da boys got to go start on Captain Eddie's boat," Marvin said as he stepped into the cockpit. "But I'd be pleased to have a drink with you."

"What's this cleanup costing me these days?" Steamer asked as he handed Marvin a beer.

"All da other boats bin payin' fifty. But I'll still do yours for forty."

"Das a damn lie!" Jimmy exclaimed as he sprang to his feet.

"Easy, Jimmy, Marvin knows better than to screw with me. Don't you, Marvin?'

"Yes sir, Captain Steamer, I said forty dollars—same's always."

Steamer finished his beer and reached into the cooler for another round. "Charlimon got any conch today?"

"Captain Steamer, I don' know 'bout dat boy. I caught him earlier hidin' back by da garage. He was all smoked up on some junk he got down on Andros last night. Let me see if I can find him." Marvin reached behind him and removed a hand-held radio from his pocket. "Charlie, Charlie, come back."

"Watchu wan, mon?" Charlie's voiced answered.

Marvin turned back to Steamer. "Imagine dat, he answered me. How many conch you want?"

"Two should be plenty."

"Charlimon, bring two conch to *War Eagle* right away."

"Thank you, Marvin," Steamer said. "Pull up a chair and help me watch the sunset. Jimmy, we still have those limes in the cooler?"

"Yes, sir, and the tabasco sauce is in the galley."

"Jimmy, you read me like a book; cold beer, cracked conch, and an island sunset. We should all be in a commercial."

The sun dissolved slowly on the horizon. Ribbons of liquid gold poured like molten lava upon the porous surface of the ink black sea. Three men sat talking quietly about baseball and weather, fishing and sex—all of the truly important topics of life. Tiny slivers of gold outlined in hues of blue and violet hung tenuously to the edge of the night sky.

Steamer leaned back into the chair and took a deep breath. The nighttime transformation was nearing completion. The warm tropical air was heavy with the aroma of boiled fish and peas 'n' rice. The muffled tones of conversation and reggae music coming from the kitchen wandered like a minstrel around the marina announcing the preparation of the evening feast. A light breeze drifted in from the southeast bearing the delicate fragrances of the sea. The aura that surrounded Steamer held him firmly in place. He was happy with his life and content to live in the here and now. It was not that he rejected the experiences of his past; it was just that who he had been and what he had done seemed to fade from his memory like passing ships in a fog.

"Captain Steamer." The brightly polished badge and buttons of Customs Officer John Murray reflected the light and glistened as he approached *War Eagle*'s berth. "May I come aboard?"

"Certainly, John. Would you join us for some cracked conch?"

"Thank you, Captain, but I think no." The officer stepped gingerly onto the cap-rail. The leather soles of his spit-shined dress shoes failed to hold on the slick surface, sending the portly gentleman tumbling most unceremoniously into the cockpit of the yacht.

"Easy, John," Steamer said as he caught the officer by the arm.

"Thank you, Captain." John Murray was obviously shaken, but pride and the official nature of his visit helped him to regain his composure quickly. "I am sorry to trouble you Captain, but I need to speak with you privately about an official matter."

Steamer looked about to ask Marvin and Jimmy to excuse them, but it was unnecessary. Both of the locals had quickly vanished. In truth, they both liked John, but it was always advisable to give the law a wide berth. "John, why don't we step inside? Here, I'll get the door." Steamer and the officer stepped inside. John took a seat at the mahogany table that served as both a dining center and a gaming table. Steamer poured two tall glasses of orange juice and joined him.

"This is in regards to the unfortunate accident you reported to me earlier today."

"John, I don't really want to get involved in that."

"I wish that it were otherwise, but a couple was apparently killed in the explosion, and that requires an official investigation. Now if you would rather, I can make arrangements for you to go to Nassau and speak with the inspectors."

"You know better than that, John," Steamer said curtly. "It's just that all that happened was that I saw the smoke. I was too far away to render any assistance so I called you on the radio. Honest, that's all I know. I really don't want to get mixed up in anyone else's trouble."

"Well, then," the officer said as he removed a series of forms and a pen from his briefcase. "Let's be done with this, and I will be on my way."

Twenty minutes later Steamer signed the last of seven documents, each stating the fact that he knew almost nothing. The customs officer packed up and departed. Steamer stood alone in the dark and remembered all the things that he hated about government and its complexities. The ship's clock chimed six bells. It was time to dress for supper.

The largest building on Shark Reef Cay was known as "The Blue Marlin." The front door was made of high-polished brass surrounding thick glass. In the main dining room the landed gentry, the owners and their guests, were seated at long, slender tables covered with starched linen. They sipped wine from fine crystal and spoke quietly of home and family, accomplishments and dreams, and plans for the long journey home. Around the back of the building, through a nondescript door, was the working man's bar. It was the realm of the boat captains and their crews. The tables were made of solid oak with none of the fancy accoutrements seen in the front of the house. This is where the men sat and held court not unlike the knights of old. The serfs and vassals had earlier busied themselves providing service between the two rooms. But now the pace had slowed, and the locals took their place in the bar with the bawdy buccaneers: the captains and their boat crews.

The knights gathered about the table—a round one, in fact. Fragments and spillage from the evening's libation lay strewn about the oaken slab. Unlike the lords and noblemen seated in the next room, these men had gained their title not through inheritance or circumstance, but through their deeds and their extraordinary prowess. They were royalty nonetheless, each in full command of his own realm. The great warriors played as hard as they worked. They had passed the evening telling grand narrative of quests and battles, damsels, and giants.

As was his custom, Steamer had dressed for supper. He wore a carefully laundered white cotton dress shirt, black slacks and shiny black cowboy boots with pointed silver tips and intricate embroidery. He had shaved and showered. He had combed his hair and the slicked wet look gave him a slightly turn-of-the-century appearance. He had intentionally waited, hoping that the commotion had settled down. The evening meal was his favorite and he hated to be rushed.

"Steamer! We were about to give up on you." Carlos Echalas was captain of the *Reel Girl*, a fifty-foot Hatteras, and was the elder statesman of the group. "*Amigo*, I've saved you a seat." Carlos was a Cuban fisherman who had escaped the brutality of his homeland and had found his niche among the boat crews of this island.

"Thanks Carlos, how'd you do today?" Steamer asked as he took the empty chair between Carlos and Dennis Chipwood, the captain of *Happy Daze*, a forty-two-foot Post.

"Had a big blue wired but he broke off at the boat. Dennis did pretty good though."

"That so?" Steamer asked as he turned his attention to the younger captain. "Talk to me son, what'd you get?"

"We got into some nice tuna. Boated six, and two wahoo. Bunch of klutzes and old women on board though, could've gotten more."

The President's voice was coming from the radio behind the bar. He was addressing a joint session of Congress but no one was listening.

"Captain Steamer," Arthur Sinclair asked "What can I get for you?"

"Evening, Arthur. I'll have a Kalik and how about run a plate by that buffet table in there for me."

"Certainly Captain, shall I charge it to the boat?" Arthur was an older man with strong features and a sincere smile.

"That'd be good, Arthur, thank you."

"Carlos, how long has Arthur been here?" Dennis asked after Arthur left.

"Do you remember when the *Atocha* sank?"

"1622, wasn't it?"

"He was here then."

"Steamer," the deep voice of Tom Langley, skipper of the *Bill Collector*, a forty-eight-foot Bertram, bellowed from the far end of the table. "Have you ever seen one of these?" The big man rolled a small chestnut down the table towards Steamer.

"What is it, Tom?" he asked as he rolled the nut over in his hand inspecting it.

"It's a magic birth control nut. Bust it open."

Steamer placed the perfectly formed chestnut on the table and smashed it with his beer bottle. To everyone's amazement, a condom which had been tightly packed inside suddenly burst open.

"That's alright, Tom. How the hell to they get those things inside and where can I get some?"

"One of the guys on the boat today was a novelty salesman says he'll send me a case of them next week. I can't wait to show one to Eddie."

"Speaking of Eddie, how'd he do today?"

Carlos took a long swig from his beer. "No work. Poor bastard hasn't had a real run for two weeks. He's scared to death the owner's going to sell *Hooker 3*. It's that boat. That run-down old Egg Harbor needs more work than Eddie's able to do. All that's happened lately is some dirty-looking goons in old fatigues from somewhere in Central America hired him to take them out to a couple of GPS waypoints and then he brought them back. They weren't interested in fishing at all. "

Arthur returned with Steamer's supper, one plate piled high with boiled fish and peas 'n' rice, and a side plate with two baked land crabs.

"Ruth sent you these special, cause she knows da bugs be your favorite."

The merriment continued all about him but Steamer tuned it out and concentrated on the culinary task that lay before him.

The evening progressed uneventfully until the loud commotion outside the door heralded the arrival of Captain Eddie Cantrell. Eddie was a small-framed man, beaten and bent by life. His thin, sandy blond hair lay tossed and greying beneath a rumpled khaki yachtsman hat. He had once again spent the day at the dock drowning his sorrows and his misfortunes in local rum.

"I can do this myself." Eddie said as he pulled away from Charlie and the other three locals who were supporting him. He reached for the door but his equilibrium had fallen victim to the rum. The door gave way as the full weight of Eddie's body crashed against it then tumbled inside.

"Come on, Eddie, we don't have time fo dis, mon. Gotta go to Andros, ya know."

"I've already told you I'm not crazy enough or drunk enough to take the bunch of you to Andros," Eddie said as Charlie and the others helped him to his feet. "Steamer," Eddie saw his friend and staggered towards the table. "Steamer, you know what this is?" Eddie held out his forearm and began to kiss and stroke it gently.

"I give up, Eddie. What is that?"

"This is the thing that I love most in life, my hide. It's true, I've become very attached to it, and these crazy bastards want me to risk it and take them to Andros just so they can drink. I say screw 'em, we can drink right here."

"It's not like that," Charlie said as he moved toward Steamer. "Dey have ladies there, fine women with dark shiny skin smoother than any silk you ever feel. Dey know what dey doin' too. Dey can reach right down inside you and hold yo soul in dey hand don cha know. Steamer, how 'bout you take us? I'll get dis one girl for you dat kin make you know how good it is to be a man."

"No hard feelings, Charlimon, but I think I'll pass."

"Eddie," Tom Langley called out. "Eddie I've got something to show you. You ever see one of these before?" Tom tossed one of the loaded nuts to Eddie.

"Sure, Tom, it's a chestnut. My father had a whole grove of them when I was growing up." Without hesitation and before anyone could stop him, Eddie popped the nut into his mouth and bit down. Even his advanced state of inebriation could not soften the shock as the latex condom exploded from its confines and inflated to full size. Eddie choked and gasped, then removed the offending article from his mouth. Horror overcame him as he realized what the rubbery substance was. For a moment he was silent. He stood there alone, coughing and spitting while everyone in the bar had a good laugh at his expense. Rage welled up inside of him; his normally fair complexion turned crimson. With one swift and decisive move Eddie drew his rigging knife from the sheath on his belt.

"You miserable bastards go ahead and laugh. Laugh all you want. I want to watch you laugh as the blood runs from your neck." Eddie's eyes were wild with anger as he slashed the knife around the room. "Go on all you bastards, laugh, 'cause when I've finished with him, I'm gonna kill every son of a bitch in this room.

"Back off Eddie," Tom said in an effort to calm him down. "No one told you to put that thing in your mouth. It was just a joke."

Steamer saw the resolve in Eddie's eyes and knew that the time for talking had passed. He stood up, centered himself, and walked cautiously toward Eddie.

"I'll kill you, you bastard!" Eddie shrieked and lunged toward Tom. Steamer moved with the swiftness of a leopard. Eddie saw him in the last instant he turned and slashed the air with the knife. But he was far too slow. Steamer delivered three rapid punches and a kick. Eddie lay motionless and bleeding.

The sudden blows to the head and the effects of the rum had rendered Eddie nearly unconscious. He lay there on the unforgiving wooden floor like an outclassed boxer waiting for the mercy of the count. The stunned occupants of the room slowly regained their composure.

Tom downed the last of his beer before he spoke. "Thanks man, I thought that crazy bastard was gonna make fish food outta me! Hell, it was only a joke. Nobody told him to eat it."

"Easy, Tom," Steamer said as he reached down to help Eddie up from the floor. "Eddie's got a lot on him right now. Help me get him back to his boat."

"Charlimon," Dennis Chipwood said, in an effort to break the tension, "tell me about this girl on Andros."

Charlie turned his attention toward the young captain. "Oh, Captain Dennis, she is like nothin' you have ever seen. She can raise you up to da top of da mountain, slowly ease you to da edge of da cliff, den ride you down, soaring thru da sky 'til ya land in da warm shimmering pool."

"Look out, Dennis, you're being hustled," said Carlos.

"Don' listen to dem. Captain Dennis with his fine yacht *Happy Daze* will be da king of Andros and da lovely ladies will serve on bended knee."

Tom's voice boomed out from across the bar. "At least make them pay for your fuel!"

Steamer and Tom supported Eddie as they walked down the dock.

"You stink, Eddie." Tom said as he gasped for air. "How long you think he's been wearing that shirt?"

Steamer was also finding it hard to stay so close to Eddie. The combination of dead fish, rum, and sweat hovered about his body like a dark cloud. Twice they had to stop and hold him while he heaved over the side of the dock. Upon reaching the stern of *Hooker 3*, the two men gently helped their stricken comrade aboard and while Tom assisted Eddie to the settee, Steamer looked about the salon of the once proud yacht. Everywhere he looked there were problems; the teakwood was dried and cracking, the carpet worn and unattended. Tools, spare parts, and fishing tackle were strewn about the salon in random fashion. Eddie's quarters were worse. All of his belongings were thrown together in a pile bespeaking the upheaval and chaos that was his life.

"What do you think Marvin would charge us to give this tub a good once over," Steamer asked as he looked inside the chart table.

"I don't know, but whatever it is, I'll pay it. I feel like I owe him that much," Tom said as he began collecting empty bottles and cans.

"You didn't cause this, Tom. It's been coming on for some time now. We'll all chip in and see if we can get him back on his feet."

"See you in the morning, Steamer." Tom said as he left the salon.

Steamer took the pistol from inside the chart table, emptied the cylinder and put the bullets in his pocket. Then he turned off the light and stepped outside.

The night air was a welcome change from the stale, unventilated cabin. Steamer jumped onto the dock and walked slowly back towards *War Eagle*. Just as he was about to step aboard he saw the single white stern light of *Happy Daze* as she cleared the piers and idled off toward the channel. The built in stereo system was cranked up, with all eight speakers pulsating to the reggae rhythms of Bob Marley.

5

Fidelity swung at anchor twenty-two miles east by southeast of the Gun Cay Channel. Small waves lapped against the port side of her fiberglass hull giving hints of the weather making up to the north. The couple emerged from the cabin light into the near darkness of nightfall. They laughed and joked and toasted their good fortune. Colin reached into the icy sludge of the cooler for two more bottles of beer. Polly stretched and sat back into the molded cockpit bench.

Colin eased himself alongside of her and kissed her cheek. She laid her head on his shoulder and patted his knee. They sat motionless as the storm approached. Time had become meaningless to them. Hours, minutes, days, were all the same to them now. They had learned to live life as it came to them. Alone on the banks they knew exactly how truly miniscule and microscopic their concerns really were.

The dying sunset to the west set the stage for the pyrotechnics firing up the northern sky. Lightning seared the sky all about them and the instantaneous thunder shook and rattled everything about them. She stood before him, ran her fingers slowly through her hair, and smiled a wry smile. "Colin, I believe it's time for us to go below." They secured the deck, climbed down the ladder into the cabin, and closed the world out as the storm raged on.

6

The grey woolen clouds buffeted the small plane about like a helpless dove. Outside the apparent wind speed approached two hundred knots, pelting the windshield with microscopic ice crystals. Jackie Morrow sat with her rosy cheek pressed against the side window a mere quarter inch away from the violent and turbulent wind that raced by. She was oblivious to the incessant drone of the propellers, or the stale odor of cigarette smoke that permeated the cockpit of the old plane. She was searching, searching for answers that seemed to always be just beyond her grasp.

Jackie's life had taken several cruel and unexplainable turns in the past two years and she was determined to take control of this situation. The investigation of her sister's death seemed mired in international red tape. All of the parties concerned were in a hurry to declare the deaths accidental and close the books on the case. But Jackie had spent several days sailing with Brenda and Wayne. She knew of his inordinate concerns for safety and she could not bring herself to believe that misfortune caused their deaths.

Through soft green eyes she tried with all her strength to cut through the gloom the enshrouded them. Jackie sat back into the seat and removed the silk scarf she had tied about her head and casually she ran her fingers through her soft auburn hair. The new shorter cut felt strange to touch but it seemed appropriate for what she had to do.

"Can we fly any lower?" she asked in a voice just loud enough to overcome the whine of the engines as the plane cruised at 6300 rpms.

"No missy," Robert Grant replied without looking away from his instruments. "It wouldn't do no good anyway. This stuff goes all da way to the deck. It won't be long though. Dis is just a small squall line. Dey are very common over the stream dis time of year. The airport at Bimini says dey got eight thousand foot ceiling. We should be out of dis in twenty minutes."

"There was an explosion on a sailboat back in April."

"Yes ma'am, I was da very first plane to spot it."

"Will we be flying anywhere near the place where it happened?"

"Yes ma'am, over da same spot."

"Would you take us as low as you came when we get there? My sister was on that boat."

"I am truly sorry ma'am. Dat was a terrible thing. Won't be much to see though. What little was left was claimed by da sea.

Jackie sat back into the seat and closed her eyes. Through the drone of the engines she could hear the soft sweet sound of her sister's voice. Music had been one of Brenda's many passions. From her earliest years songs had danced from her lips like clear mountain water bubbling up from an endless spring. She sang and danced in school functions, K through 12. Her delicate soothing voice had been featured by church choirs and glee clubs throughout southern Connecticut. During her college years Brenda had tried to sing professionally as lead vocalist with several local bands but her unusual talent did not readily lend itself to mixing boards and complex instrumentation. Finally, she tried the coffee houses for a while, working solo with her voice and an acoustic guitar.

Brenda met Wayne in April of her junior year. He took her sailing on the cool waters of Long Island Sound, Block Island Sound, and up the beautiful Connecticut River. Realization had come to her on a beautiful summer day just two miles north of Essex. The riggings of the small sloop hummed and rattled and kept time as the boat neared the tree line on the east bank. The wind blew across the tightly stretched sail and whistled up through soft fragrant evergreens that towered above the river. All at once she found herself swept away by the rhythms and the song lines and the harmony of the universe. Softly she hummed and tapped, then burst forth in song:

> *Gently flow the sparkling waters*
> *From the mountains to the sea*
> *Softly sing the minstrel wind song*
> *As she dances with the trees*
> *Leafy blankets wrap the mountains*
> *To protect them from the cold*
> *My gift is for the earth song*
> *It will nevermore be sold.*

Jackie felt the warm sunlight on her face and slowly opened her eyes. Her sister's song played one more time in her subconscious. Torn between waking and sleeping, her mind clung to the fading memory.

Four thousand feet below, tiny ships bobbed about in the frothy sea. Wakes left by speedy sport fishing boats appeared as small white arrows drawn on a textured grey slate.

"Not a good day to be crossing the stream by boat," Robert said as he turned his attention to the GPS.

Six small bubbles suddenly caught Jackie's attention and she leaned against the window for a better view. The first two bubbles were blue and yellow, one was red, white and blue, and the rest were solid white. A flotilla of sleek racing yachts was running before the wind with a full spinnaker set. Instinctively, she reached behind her.

"Skipper, look!" she had almost said aloud. Then she saw tan and white as the crystal clear water danced across the rippling sands of the Great Bahamas Banks.

High above, Jackie rocked in pain as wave after wave of memories crashed in upon her. "If they had only known, but how could they?" Skipper had complained of feeling achy and feverish most of the day. They started not to let him play. But this was his last game and it seemed so important to him. After his shower the young boy shivered with the chills of a high fever. Jackie gave him two aspirins and kissed him good night. Only once did they hear him cough. The rare virus silently strained his heart beyond its capacity. At approximately two o'clock in the morning, Skipper Morrow died in his sleep. Jackie looked up and he wasn't there and the world went on as if he never had been. She could not let the same thing happen to Brenda!

"Lower, please!" she insisted. "I would like for you to get me as close as you can to the place where my sister's boat burned."

"Yes ma'am," Robert gave up his attempts at pleasantries. Flying with this single-minded and headstrong woman was as difficult as trying to please General Santiago and his lunatic lieutenant.

He banked right and began to descend to one thousand feet. As the small plane lost altitude Jackie became more and more aware of their forward speed.

They were flying through time and space, over and into a land that longed to cover up and smooth over the deaths of these unfortunate sailors, just as it had done for centuries past.

"I don't see anything!" It was almost a plea.

"It was over der." Robert pointed just to the right of the deep water near Northwest Channel Light.

Jackie prayed and searched hoping to find something that no one else could have. She imagined seeing Brenda bobbing safety in a life jacket and waving frantically. But there was nothing but an uninhabited spit of land called Spinner Cay. She looked for clues, something that would lead her to the discovery of her sister alive and well. But there was only the abandoned decaying tower of North-west Channel Light. In the end she looked for a remnant, some small item that would tell her that her sister had once been at this barren place. But all she saw were the rippling sand bars shifting and changing beneath the surface of the sea.

Robert slowly increased the pressure on his rudder pedals, then turned the yoke ever so gently north. Hy-draulic fluid pumped like life blood beneath the metallic wings, ailerons pressed against powerful air currents. Robert lined the plane up for his final approach to Shark Reef Cay. Landing from this angle would be more difficult than normal, but well within his capabilities. Besides, Robert always welcomed a challenge. A troublesome gust of wind swept across the surface of the sea, then up onto the runway. Quick reaction and steel nerves averted the danger. Clouds of dust and sand erupted from beneath the wheels as the plane touched down on the narrow dirt runway. Within minutes pilot and passenger stepped first into the white heat of tropical mid-day, then into the plush air-conditioned comfort of the customs office.

7

Customs officer John Murray buttoned each of the polished brass buttons of his uniform jacket as if each one was a metal or a battle ribbon. He was proud of his position with the government and even though there was no requirement that he do so, he always wore his dress uniform to and from his office. His normal routine called for him to wear one pair of shoes for three days then switch to the identical pair of shiny black oxfords. On Sunday he would shine both pairs as well as polish the brass buttons of his jacket.

But the week was not normal and it seemed that his routine would be endlessly interrupted. This was only Tuesday and he had already heard from Nassau (New Providence) four times. Although he had the highest respect for the government, he did not enjoy talking to his superiors and he detested the additional work that each phone call generated. There was a smudge on the toe of his left shoe. No time, the woman waiting for him in his office had required the pilot to ring him twice already.

John grabbed his second pair of shoes, downed a banana and some guava juice, and hurried out the door. Ignoring the oppressive heat, he stepped briskly along the pathway that led to his office at the airport. He rounded the bend and stopped short in amazement. Charlie Baxter sat cross-legged in the center of the sandy roadbed nursing a bottle of coconut rum.

"Dis is what I really needed dis mornin'. Charlimon, what are ya doin in the middle of the runway?"

Charlie took a long sip from the rum bottle and looked around.

"De air-port, de air-port, mon how can you call dis an airport? Ain't nuttin here 'cept a dirt road and dat shanty yo call an office."

"I don't have time for you today, Charlimon. Look at chu, not even noon and you already stinking drunk. I'm going to find Mr. Webster later and suggest he fire you."

As John walked off, Charlie tried to stand up. He had been waiting to talk to the custom officer for most of the morning. Charlie felt strange, his body out of control. The cocaine within him caused his mind to swirl shifting at high speed from one thought to another. But the rum held him down. Physically he could not stand and his speech was slurred.

"Murray, got to talk to yo 'bout the commandos. Dey got the girl."

"Go home, Charlimon, go home and sleep it off. The commandos are gone and good riddance to 'em." John said without looking back.

"But, my brudda on Andros told me...."

"Das a good idea, call yo brudda, maybe he could use anudda drunk on Andros." With the words spoken, John Murray opened the door and stepped into the coolness of his air-conditioned office.

Jackie stood up as John entered the room.

Anger brought Charles Baxter to the brink of madness. With all of the intensity of a newborn colt, Charlie struggled to stand.

"Damn! Why won't nobody listen to me? I need to tell 'em. Jimmy said Steamer saw the smoke from the boat. Maybe Steamer will listen."

Charlie staggered off to find Steamer.

8

"I told ya, Steamer, Hopalong Cassidy was the greatest cowboy," said Jimmy. The name sounded strange in his Bahamian lilt.

"He's not real, he's an actor. Now Wyatt Earp was a real cowboy and was the greatest ever." The round robin wheelhouse discussion took yet another turn when they were interrupted by the blare of the VHF radio.

"Customs office calling *War Eagle*." Mr. Murray's voice bellowed out loud and clear.

"*War Eagle*, standing by," answered Steamer.

"Captain Causey, could you come to my office right away?" Mr. Murray sounded large and in charge, and not to be trifled with.

"I'll come right now," Steamer answered. "I wonder what he wants?" Jimmy shrugged and Steamer climbed down from the flying bridge and walked across the island to the airport. Steamer was not happy. He didn't like dealing with the government and he hated being summoned over the radio.

By the time Steamer arrived at the airport customs office, sweat was beginning to trickle down his shirt. The old rusty window unit was running at top speed frantically wailing against the heat. He knocked and stepped inside.

Customs Officer Jack Murray sat behind his massive desk, pristine with everything in its place. Across from him was seated the most stunning woman Steamer had ever seen. Her short-cropped auburn hair set off her creamy white shoulders and her long lanky arms. She wore a light cotton flowered sundress and she smelled like honeysuckle and roses.

"Miss Jackie, this is Captain Steamer Causey. He is the man who reported the unfortunate incident."

Steamer started to recoil and deny any involvement but just then Jackie uncrossed her legs and stood to greet him and that small glimpse of her thigh caused his world to turn and sealed his fate.

"Steamer, your boss, Mr. Bailey, has asked us to assist Miss Jackie in any way we can." Officer Jack Murray went on incessantly about Jackie and her sister and how Steamer could be of service. Steamer hardly listened. All he could do was watch Jackie. She was young, athletic, and smart. "Classy" was the word he was looking for. She was classy to the nines. At one moment she looked soft and vulnerable, then with a change of expression she look like she could drop you where you stood.

"You could take her around and talk to people..." Murray said, and punctured the statement with his hands.

"Well, if Mr. Bailey asked, I am obliged to help. I'm sure we can find out something. Would you care to join me for supper to discuss this further?"

"I would, Captain, but I already accepted Mr. Murray's invitation."

Steamer quickly cut his eyes over at Jack Murray who was smiling the biggest smile he had ever seen the black man smile.

"Well, tomorrow then," Steamer said as he stood to leave.

Steamer was mad and confused. He had committed to something he didn't want to get mixed up in, yet he had done so for a chance to get to know this woman, only to be snaked, by of all people, Jack Murray. Steamer was walking back toward the boat when he saw a white suit disappear into the bar. In what would prove to be a momentous course change, he followed.

The furniture inside the bar was primitive but varnished to a brilliant shine. The air smelled of aftershave and cigar smoke. Cuban Louie adjusted his girth and settled into his favorite captain's chair.

"*Qué pasa*, Louie," Steamer said as he walked up behind him.

"Life is good," Louie answered as the bartender brought him a mojito. Louie gestured for Steamer to join him. Steamer ordered a shot of dark rum, neat, and joined him at the bar.

"My friend, what do you know of these commandos? All I know is rumors from a rather unreliable source but it may be important to someone I know."

"They are very bad men. They are *estúpido* and un-disciplined but *peligroso, muy peligroso*."

"How are they dangerous?"

"They believe that their cause is just and that anyone who gets in the way ... *muerto!*" He slid his thumb across his throat for effect. They are not really military, they only wear the uniforms. Stay far, far away from them, *mi amigo*."

"Louie, what do you know about the sailboat fire?"

"It is a very sad story, my friend. A young couple from Chicago came down here to charter a boat." Louie looked around the bar then drew on his cigar. "They were given the wrong boat. That *bastardo* General Santiago had some secret deal working that involved that boat." He sipped his drink slowly. "He had been hanging around all week waiting for something. When he saw the boat leave early and go the wrong direction he thought he had been double-crossed. He did not wait for explanation; he pounced like a lion. *Estúpido, muy estúpido*. Boat gone, innocent people gone, all gone, such a waste."

Steamer knocked back the rest of his rum and slapped Louis on the back, thanking him, and walk back to the boat. He was almost to the dock when he caught a glimpse of Jackie crossing the runway on her way back to the condo. Then in an instant she was gone, yet he was sure he could still smell her perfume.

9

It was almost ten when Jackie arrived at the fuel dock. She was wearing jeans, a plaid shirt and running shoes that gave her quite the athletic look. Jimmy and Steamer had just finished fueling *War Eagle*.

"Wait, Miss! I will help you aboard," said Jimmy in his most gracious of tones.

"Jackie, this is Jimmy. My right hand man," said Steamer.

"So pleased to meet you," said Jackie.

"The pleasure is all mine." Jimmy extended his arm.

"So, Captain Causey. Tell me all you know."

"Please call me Steamer. Let's step into the cabin where it's cooler. Jimmy, warm her up and get her ready for sea."

"Yes, Captain."

Steamer and Jackie talked in private for about an hour before they got under way.

War Eagle jumped up onto a plane and began dancing through the swells. The only way to Bear's bar was northeast around Shark Reef Cay, then a thirty-mile slog up the windward side of the Berry Islands. Steamer tacked as best he could in a near futile effort to find a comfortable heading.

"Bear is a piece of work," he said to Jackie. The volume and cadence of his voice fluctuated as he adjusted to the wind noise and the drone of the engines.

"He used to be married to a fire-breathing redhead that took him for all he had. She cleaned him out when she and her boyfriend left. Then she got a high-priced lawyer to get whatever was left. One day Bear got his paycheck and it was short by three hundred dollars of what the court had ordered him to pay. He had no hope for making up the difference. It wasn't enough money to stay but it was sure enough to leave. He cashed it and bought a ticket to anywhere. 'Anywhere' turned out to be the engine room of a Norwegian-flagged cruise ship that ran out of Miami. He met a sweet girl bartender on the ship that helped him put the bar together. He married her and they live somewhere down on Frazier Cay."

Steamer turned to put the sea more kindly on his stern but the wind lifted the exhaust.

"Is there any way of getting free of these fumes?" Jackie asked as she moved about the flying bridge.

"We have to live with this for a few minutes until we get around Petite Cay. Anyway, the ship he was on anchored up twice a week in that cove at Great Stirrup

Cay on the north end of the Berry Islands. One day Bear was walking out on deck and he got a glimpse of an old abandoned hotel that sits on Cistern Cay. The place got wiped out during hurricane Andrew. He suddenly had a plan and for the next few years he scrounged around for what he needed then one day he moves in and sets up shop. The bar was an instant success. Off-duty crewmen from the ships that anchor there began patronizing him in an effort to escape all the tourists from Ohio. Then the locals would drop by with their tip money after the ships got underway. Add in a few more informed fishermen, and he had the makings of one first class island bar."

"How did he ever get the means and the permission to do all that?" she asked as she settled back into her seat. Steamer had rounded the point now and was headed more westerly.

"I doubt he ever asked anyone. It had to have taken many trips to sneak what he need onto the island. Once he got established, everyone just accepted him. Besides, you haven't seen the place yet: it's pretty much just a pile of cinderblocks with a roof, sort of. It's just the other side of that small cay over there," Steamer said as he pointed to an almost deserted island just south of the lighthouse at Little Stirrup. "We'll duck in just below the light and thread the needle into the cove."

"And tell me again just why we have to come here?"

"Because this is a working man's bar and if anyone inside of a hundred miles of this place knows anything about your sister it has been discussed in here. And I have learned that whatever Bear tells you, you can take it to the bank. The trick is to get him to tell you anything."

Steamer stood at the controls and had Jimmy climb out onto the bow pulpit to spot for him. He began paying considerably more attention as he slowed War Eagle and began picking his way through the shallow water channel. Jackie stood beside him in silence, marveling at his skill. Steamer thought about going to anchor and being ferried in but that just wasn't his style and besides he had already committed to the channel. The dock outside Bear's Bar had not been completed with the same designs or materials with which it had begun. In fact, to the untrained observer it didn't look finished at all. War Eagle hogged the entire south side. Steamer and Jimmy scurried about securing lines and checking the fenders.

"How's she laying, Jimmy?" Steamer asked.

"She'll do, Captain," Jimmy yelled from the dock. He did not like this escapade. He was the best striker on the finest charter boat in all the islands and he missed fishing. He decided that for now he would just stay aboard. He had seen all the shanty island bars he cared to see. Bimini would be better. There was no shore power to be had, so Steamer left the genset running and told Jimmy to keep an eye on it. On the lee side of the island the trade winds had died and the afternoon heat had become oppressive. Steamer and Jackie stepped gingerly onto the dock and walked up the narrow path to the bar.

Bear sat alone at the end of the bar talking to Tony Lind. T.L. was the biggest, strongest black man Steamer had ever met, and T.L. and Bear were the best of friends. The remembrances of stale beer and last night's cigars lingered in the eddy just below the window air conditioner. The unit was old and originally of German build. The effort to keep the noisy old clunker running had been heroic. There were so many scavenged parts that original designer would never have recognized it. But it did the job, barely. Nothing known to man could really overcome the tropical heat, but everyone tried.

Jackie and Steamer walked through the door and stood motionless as their eyes adjusted. With one look Jackie instantly knew why they called him Bear. He was a big, strong man with sloping shoulders and rounded features. A full black beard just beginning its turn to gray hid dark, determined eyes. A small gold earring, a tattoo and a headband completed the look. Bear sat in all his glory looking ever so much the pirate that he was.

"The park rangers haven't caught up with you yet?" Steamer joked.

"Oh gee, I haven't heard that one in a while," Bear retorted sarcastically. "The latest one is 'Hi, I'm Jim. Marlin is waiting in the truck with the camera crew.'"

"How you been, Bear?"

"Just another shitty day trapped in paradise. How 'bout you?"

"SSDD."

"SSDD?"

"Yeah, same shit, different day." Steamer led Jackie to the barstools alongside the one that Bear had claimed. Jackie passed on the cigar, but had little choice but to drink a beer.

"Cubans and Kalik, does it ever get any better than this?" Bear lit his cigar, took a long draw, and leaned back to exhale.

"Greater truth was never spoken," Steamer said as he took the lighter from the bar and lit his cigar. "Speaking of Cubans, I saw Cuban Louie the other day." Bear just smiled but had no other response to that.

"T.L., what happened to you?" Steamer noticed that this monster of a man had cuts and contusions all about his head and face. Bear laughed a deep bellowing laugh.

"Yea, T.L., tell Steamer about stupid night."

"Cap'n, it was awful. My partner an' me was in da bar on Andros and a fight started. My partner patted his pistol in his pocket and said, 'Let's end this.' Den he stood up, pulled his pistol, and began wavin' it about. It was awful cap'n, as he said 'don't nobody move,' the cylinder drop outta the gun, an' roll across da flo. Da whole bar jumped us." Everyone but T.L. laughed. The big man just shook his head and walked off.

"Bear, this is Jackie Morrow. Her sister and brother-in-law were on that boat that blew up a few months ago."

"Pleased to meet ya, m'lady. So sorry for your loss." Bear's entire attitude suddenly changed and he became guarded and detached.

Jackie leaned over to Bear, "Could I see your tattoo?" The big man lifted the sleeve of his t-shirt over his bulging bicep and there was a most handsome anchor with a ship's wheel and a crucifix superimposed.

"It's protected me through a lot of tight spots, little lady. I can tell you that."

"The problem is, Bear," Steamer leaned in closer so as not to be over heard, "they never found her body, only his."

"Sharks?" whispered Bear.

"No idea," countered Steamer. "BASRA was there fairly quickly and since then we have heard a lot of rumors about the commandos."

"You don't want to mess with those boys. They're seriously bad guys."

"What do you know about them, Bear?"

"They're from Nicaragua. Their headquarters are on a small island off the north coast. They're not recognized by the government or anyone else for that matter, and they have no military training. They're just a bunch of ideological potheads who think the world owes them a living, but they're seriously dangerous. Do you think they have her?"

"That's why we're here. You hear anything?"

"Just rumors and macho bullshit. They think they were double-crossed somehow and that people would pay." He moved closer to Steamer and whispered, "They were braggin' that they had a hostage and that she was *muy hermosa*. If I hear anything else I'll get word up to you. But Steamer, be careful. That girl is more than likely dead by now."

They rejoined Jackie, drank a few beers, told some old sea stories, then said their goodbyes.

Within the hour they were in open ocean, cruising east by south.

"Where to now?" asked Jackie.

"I need to go find Tadda."

"Who?"

"Tadda. He's the only one I know that's crazy enough to go to Nicaragua with us."

"We're going where?!" said Jackie in alarm.

10

Windward Cay drifts through time and space in pristine stillness, void of human footprints save those of the lovers anchored in the cove. Hard packed grains of sand lay baking in the merciless tropical sun. A white land crab stands near the water's edge delicately lifting alternating legs as if he could bear the heat no longer.

Tadda's girlfriend Dallas sat bathing in the warm shallow water near the sandy beach of the deserted cay. With long soft strokes she shaved her shapely tanned legs. With a practiced gentle touch her hand followed the path of the razor. Although the motion allowed her to check for stubble, she had found that the touch also eased the burning sensation brought on as salt water bathed her razor-chafed skin. She could have gotten by with less irritation: Tadda would never have asked this of her, but he was so fiercely proud of her beauty and always loved the feel of her smooth-shaven legs. There was nothing she wouldn't do to please him.

The long-legged beauty rolled over and lay spread-eagle face down in the warm clear water. A small blue and yellow damselfish swam towards her. Dallas reached out to touch the curious creature, but her motion sent the once brave damselfish scampering for safety. She lay there with her chin resting on her hands, her face elevated just above the surface. "This is so different," she thought, "lying naked in the sun, cloaked only by the natural beauty of the world, and none but the fish, the birds, and my beloved Tadda to share my joy."

Dallas no longer thought of her childhood. She repressed the frightening details of life in the peasant village of her Cuban homeland. Those memories belonged to a child, a beautiful child who was forced to trade her innocence and her purity for a chance to escape the poverty and oppression of Havana and the slums of Miami. She now lay in the warm, protected water and shivered with the memories.

The wind blew unchecked across the surface of the unsettled sea, across the desolate sandbars of the Dry Tortugas, then across the small feet and frail legs of a lost little girl. She had left Cuba with her family when she was eleven years old. She had only half-listened as her father and two uncles planned their escape. Dreams of endless wealth and freedom were foreign to her, and she was a piece of human flotsam in their desperate plan.

Fourteen people had boarded the ugly little "chug" under the cloak of darkness. Three families had crammed everything they could into the boat. They bet their lives and the lives of those they loved on one shot at the dream of wealth and freedom they had dared to believe in. From the start, confusion and chaos took control of the frail craft and its piteous human cargo. She stayed low and helped bail slimy water from around the base of the noisy, smelly, and fuming automobile engine. She never saw the advancing wave that destroyed her future. She didn't see the looks of anguish turning into stark terror on the faces of her parents as they were torn from the boat and vanished into the sea.

With the massive brick structure that is Fort Jefferson looming in the background, a group of men in an indistinguishable array of uniforms processed the survivors. The men in uniform were attempting to fend off a small contingent of onlookers, passengers aboard the daily ferry from Key West. But she was alone. Alone at the edge of an unknown sea in an unknown land and confronted with an unknown future.

Then she heard a dog bark in the distance. Instinctively, she looked up. The spray that flew from her paws looked like sparks in the sunlight as Salty charged along the water's edge, leaving her owner, the ferry captain, trailing far behind. The young labrador retriever was in full stride, her soft yellow fur glistened with sea water, her long legs driving her on in excited anticipation of her favorite game of "get the stick." They were less than fifty feet apart when their eyes met. The child and the dog, both on the edge of adolescence, both on the edge of the sea, both on the edge of life. With the boundless enthusiasm of the puppy that she was, Salty ran toward the child. The eleven-year-old girl opened her arms, and her heart, and buried her face in the familiar and not-unpleasant scent of wet dog. Salty licked her face and tickled her ear with a wet brown nose and was treated to a tummy rub in return.

The child's delighted laughter was the first sound she made in America. Time and dark memories temporarily vanished as the two played on the beach. They rolled in the sand with giggles and wags. Soon they quieted down and collapsed together in a heap. For a single moment, soft golden eyes met black ones and spoke volumes in the language that only children and puppies know.

Captain Rick's whistle was heard only by Salty. A last slow look between child and dog, and one more wag of the tail, and her work was done. Salty raced back to her owner. The child stood and gathered up her meager belongings. She stopped briefly, smiled a little toward the retreating puppy, then looked seaward and was finally able to cry.

"Things will be better in America." For ten years she lived in the slums of Miami. Lately she had been cleaning hotel rooms by day and dancing by night in the dark, smoke-filled clubs that exist on the periphery of acceptable nightlife. For years she danced on stage staring back into the fat drunken faces of perversion. She prostrated herself before nameless men who valued her nakedness at two dollars or less.

Now Dallas shook her head, clearing her mind of all unpleasantness. She was here now, with Tadda, with all she ever needed or wanted. She returned the razor to the camera bag she used for her toiletries, strapped the bag around her waist and swam back to the boat. Tadda was gone now, diving for their breakfast as he had done every morning of the two years they had been together. Dallas lifted herself onto the diving platform, then climbed aboard. Tiny water droplets clung to her skin causing her long thin torso to shine in the morning sunlight.

The *Donwanna* was a strange craft. During the years that the old boat had worked as a long-liner, a large storage box stretched across the stern. The box had been used to store hooks and line and buoys. Dallas had magically transformed this deep bin into a bountiful garden. Tadda took some money from a small job he had done in Nassau and bought potting soil, seeds and fertilizer. The bin was now alive with succulent fruits, fresh vegetables, aromatic herbs and a few small cannabis plants. Dallas reached into the dense foliage and picked several ripe cherry tomatoes. She placed them in a bowl on the table.

As he had done every morning, Tadda had prepared for her return. On the table lay a colorful new shell, a fresh coconut quartered and husked, its milky renderings saved in a glass jar, a clean folded towel and a pail of fresh water warming in the sun. Dallas lifted the polished shell of the giant whelk ablaze with hues of yellow, red, and brown. The shells marked their time together and each one was a cherished memory. She took the jar of coconut milk and poured the silky liquid through her long dark hair. Squeezing the fresh pulp like a sponge she rubbed the fragrant oil across her face and neck, across her shoulders and down her dark brown arms. She prepared a fresh piece, closed her eyes and gently rubbed the milky pulp around and across her petite breasts and down her flat, toned stomach. With the last two sections she massaged her legs and feet. Taking a washcloth from the bottom of the pail, she began rinsing the salt and the coconut oil from her face and body. With every stroke she washed away her fears, her worries, her past. With the pail tilted above her head she rinsed the conditioning coconut milk from her hair. She needed a towel to dab the water from her eyes. She looked up and there he was.

Her funny little fisherman looked like a picture from a *National Geographic* magazine. Tadda was standing on the deck naked, his tanned leathery skin dripping wet. To make up for the disadvantage of Tadda's diminutive height, God had anointed him with an extra helping of manhood. In one hand he held his fins and mask. In the other he held a spear with two yellowtail snappers impaled near the tip.

"Did you get the tomatoes?" he said with a broad smile

"How long have you been watching me?" she teased.

"Long enough to break out in a cold sweat. I'd better get breakfast cooking before I forget how." He tossed the equipment on the deck, took the bowl of tomatoes from the table and announced, "Boiled fish, and peas 'n' rice in thirty minutes." Tadda went to the galley and Dallas climbed the ladder to her favorite perch atop the wheelhouse. She tightly rolled the towel into a pillow, retrieved her favorite hat and lay down on the soft warm teakwood pallet that her love had built for her.

With a time-tested adjustment of the soft gray corduroy baseball cap, she shaded her cool green eyes. Dallas was amazed at how fulfilling and uncomplicated life had become. This simple fisherman provided for her every need. She in turn pleasured him in ways he could never have imagined. She closed her eyes and thought of his smile. The smile he wore the first night he had walked into the club.

He had just completed his last run aboard the long-line fishing boat *Hombre*. He had saved enough money to buy his own old long-liner and equip it for commercial diving—and in celebration, the crew had decided he needed a night on the town. Just before eleven, the group of rowdy revelers found their way to the "Body Shop."

Dallas stepped on stage at eleven. As she danced she found herself strangely attracted to the funny little man. He had a broad smile and eyes that sparkled. Something was different. While other men fixated their gaze on her exposed body, Tadda stared deeply into her eyes. Before the night was through the crewmen bought Tadda a table dance. He chose Dallas and as she danced for him alone a spark was ignited deep within their souls. For the first time ever she did not want the music to end. When the dance was over, she sat and talked with him. As they talked, Tadda began to gently rub her back.

Tadda returned to the club three more times that week. His lavishing of attention and their mutual attraction made it difficult for Dallas to work and by the end of the week the club manager replaced her. As timing would have it, Tadda was waiting for her in the parking lot.

"I've got a dive job over on Nassau," he said in a tentative and pleading voice. "I'd like for you to come wit' me. I only got two hunret dollars I kin give you, but it won't cost ya nuthin' and we'd only be gone a week or two."

Two weeks, two years, the lovers drifted through their own idyllic paradise. When the need for more money arose, as it did from time to time, Tadda would put into the nearest inhabited island. There was always work for a commercial diver of his caliber. A load of fuel, fresh water, rice, dried peas, Tabasco sauce, and a night on the town with his lady, then back to the uninhabited cays and islands that were their retreat. They looked the part of the gypsies they had become. Tadda paid far more attention to Dallas than he did to his rusty old boat. All he ever asked of *Donwanna* is that she float and run.

Dallas could hear him now milling about in the galley. The clinking of pans and plates mingled with the aroma of the spicy fish and rice that floated up to greet her. Without warning, Tadda's face appeared at the top of the ladder.

"Breakfast is served," he said as he one-handed the large tray of food over the handrail.

"I could have come down," she said.

"No need, m'dear, I am here."

Seated on the edge of the pallet, the couple enjoyed their simple meal at the leisurely pace that had become rhythm of their life. As they ate, Tadda once again began to tell her stories from his childhood. Stories of fishing, and hunting, and general mischief as he grew to manhood on the barrier islands of the North Carolina coast. Dallas loved these happy stories of youth. Just then something he said made her remember her friend, Helena. She re-membered two young girls walking along a white sand beach near Varadero on the north coast of Cuba. Helena and Carmen ... funny that Tadda had never asked about her real name.

The forked scraped across his dish as Tadda scooped the last piece of the savory fish and offered it to Dallas. As he slid the fork from her mouth tiny ribbons of the spicy sauce dribbled down her chin. He reached over, wiped her chin then kissed her softly, and gently lowered her back to her pillow. Dishes removed, he watched as the love of his life stretched out on the soft wood before him. He lay down beside her and with an easy fluid motion they melted together. Their bodies and souls entwined in the primal dance of love.

For over an hour they slept, wrapped safely in each other's arms. Dallas was the first to wake. The wind had changed direction, coming now from the southwest. The smells of the ocean were different from that direction. The wind carried the scent of development, civilization, and humanity. She slipped out of his sleeping embrace, sat up and listened. There was a sound. An unexplainable sense of panic and fear welled up within her. There it was again. The vibrations of the approaching engines carried a sense of urgency, carried dark memories from her past. A boat was coming; the world was coming, coming for them. For the first time in two years she felt naked and vulnerable. Dallas went below, put on a white cotton shirt and a pair of cut-off jeans, then returned and woke Tadda.

"That's just Steamer," he said, as he lowered his binoculars. "I wonder what that old goat wants."

He would find out in a few short moments. Steamer expertly maneuvered *War Eagle* alongside the old steel-hull's vessel. Tadda and Dallas assisted in securing the lines, and within minutes the four were seated on the *Donwanna* is enjoying a cold beer.

"Tadda, I have a problem. As best I can determine, Jackie's sister has been kidnapped by the so-called commandos. It appears they're holding her in Nicaragua. We need to go down and see about her. And we can't take *War Eagle*. She's too flashy and she doesn't belong to me."

"So you want me to risk my boat instead."

"No, it's not like that. You're the only good guy I know that has a boat that can make this trip, and I can't think of anyone better to have my back."

"I won't endanger Dallas."

"I've already thought of that. I know a guy, Elon, who has a small rental bungalow on Bimini where she can stay until we get back. We should be gone at the most two or three weeks."

Dallas wanted to argue but she knew that it would be futile. Pleasantries exchanged, they agreed to meet in Bimini the beginning of the next week. Dallas stepped quickly below. She was visibly upset. Jackie and Steamer climbed aboard *War Eagle* and headed out.

"Where are we going now?" Jackie asked.

"To Great Harbor Cay. I've got to speak to Elon. You'll enjoy it though: tonight is Lobster Fest."

Twilight lingered as if it were sad that the affair had not begun on its watch. All the principals were now in play. Bright colorful tents, erected earlier in the day, were being filled with tables and wares. Every tent proudly displayed the name of the proprietor. Two young boys set up the sound system under the watchful and often critical eyes of their elders. Their jobs completed, they gathered about the makeshift bar making sure that the golden Kalik was at its coldest. Small children helped their mothers set up the feasts. Steamer and Jackie strolled about mingling with the tapestry of humanity that now approached the gathering. He removed his hand from her waist as he introduced himself to an Afghani woman and her two children. When she reached for him again he ducked away.

"Jackie, I need to go find Elon. Meet me back by the jewelry tent in about half an hour," Steamer said as he stepped out into the darkness.

Sunset waned to full dark, and with all the fanfare due this momentous occasion, the music shook the old worn speakers and the party began. Jackie strolled from tent to tent, greeting smiles with smiles.

She was reaching for a small shell bracelet when he returned.

"Did you find who you were looking for?"

"Yeah, Elon has a place over in Bimini that he will let Dallas use until we get back. He told me a lot more about the commandos."

"What did he say?"

"I'll fill you in later. Let's enjoy the festival."

They sampled everything; conch fritters, lobster salad, boiled cassava root, grouper fingers, all the delicacies of this island paradise.

They watched two small children dancing and bent down to greet them. A small girl with her hair bound tightly in colorful ribbons reached up for Steamer and began to dance. A thin old man dressed in his finest shirt and dress slacks moved toward them. His soft white beard shown against his weathered dark skin; his eyes sparkled with mischief. Suddenly he too began to dance. He danced with the grace and balance of a man many years his younger. The dance spread like the fragrance of an orchid on the wind. Soon everyone danced. Then a man took the microphone and asked everyone to give him their attention. "Let's start this da right way," he said. "Let us sing our national anthem." Softly and lovingly, the small group of humanity isolated on this small sandy island joined their hearts with all their countrymen and sang of the wonders of this country.

A sharp whistle and a drum, and the rag-tag band began the Junkanoo parade. Every imaginable size and type of drum and whistle and bell came together in the song of the soul. The music was alive and unfettered. Everyone fell in line and danced along the road that bordered the marina. They danced uphill and down. They danced around the bar and back down to the water. They danced until their hearts had joined with all that were there. As they danced, the borders and boundaries that separate and enslave people began to melt away like the ice cubes in their drinks.

Unlike its beginning, the parade ended softly and slowly. As if they were children at play, the group gradually lost focus and one by one they moved on to other adventures. Steamer and Jackie strolled along the docks, admiring the boats and speaking to the latecomers who were only now meandering toward the festival. The music had gone back to the prerecorded version. It was still quite lively with all the rhythm and all the dreams of the islands. But the intensity was now muffled by distance and by the water. Jackie stopped at the edge of the dock and looked over the side. There were dozens of small fish swimming along the edge of stone seawall. She knelt and gracefully folded her beautiful legs beneath her. He watched her as he always did. She looked up at him and smiled. She reached her hand for him and he helped her up. They sipped the last of their beer and strolled back to the boat. As he waited for her to clear the ladder he looked up. The Pleiades, the "Seven Sisters," were smiling down upon them.

The festival ended shortly after midnight but the music and the reverie mixed with the scents of all the exotic leftovers drifted out across the banks.

11

Rust-mottled steel rushed through crystalline water as the *Donwanna* ran through the narrow cut at Gun Cay Channel. Tadda had pushed the tired old engines to their limits. His nerves were frayed as well. Eight hours of slugging his way across the shallow waters of the Great Bahamas Banks, meticulously picking his way through the ever-changing unmarked channel that led from Northwest Channel Light to the Gun Cay Pass, had taken its toll, and Tadda was exhausted.

Dallas offered to go with him to Nicaragua, and he would have given anything to have her by his side, but he would not risk her safety. Still, his soul would not be soothed. He wanted this journey done and behind him. He wanted to go back to his quiet life with his love.

But there was a code amongst those who lived "down island." "Don't refuse and don't abuse." He knew Steamer lived by the code and wouldn't have asked if he had another way. That knowledge was not of much help as he rounded marker at Gun Cay Channel and broke into the deep blue water of the Atlantic. There was something ominous about the wind and waves out here on the unprotected sea. Tadda drew a long breath and sat back.

"How 'bout a beer, love?" he said as he turned North by Northeast, and ran alongside the beautiful rock formations that define the western limits of the banks.

""Here you are," Dallas said as she handed him a cold one, with a fresh squeeze of sour orange in it. "To a big night in Bimini," she said as she clinked their bottles together in a toast.

Tadda smiled and brought the golden brew to his lips. Tomorrow he would think of Steamer and the plans for the passage. Tonight belonged to Dallas and, beginning with this beer, there would be no further distractions.

They tied *Donwanna* up at the concrete wall near the seaplane terminal. They walked north along the dirt road called Queen Anne's Highway. Steamer had made arrangements for Dallas to stay in a bungalow until they returned, but tonight she would remain on the boat. She reached down to pick up a shell, looked up and smiled at him.

"Gonna be a hell of a night," said Tadda, returning her smile.

Pure white limestone sand crunched beneath their feet as the lovers walked hand in hand down the middle of Queen Anne's Highway. As they passed the Bimini Big Game Club, the bright yellow seaplane from Brown's

Aviation buzzed closely overhead on its approach to the lagoon. The gateway to the Banks was as busy as ever. He moved his hand to her waist and pulled her towards him. She reached her arm around behind him and snuggled her head upon his shoulder. She wore cutoff jeans, sandals, and an oversized white cotton dress shirt that had once belonged to her father. He looked at her in amazement. She was as exciting to him dressed as she was naked. He loved to watch her move.

They pushed open the heavy wooden door and walked into The Compleat Angler. Hemingway's old house on Bimini had long ago been converted into the kind of museum Papa would have wanted. The small clapboard house was now the busiest bar in town. The lovers settled onto high stools at the end of the big oak bar and ordered the first of many beers. The Angler supported tables for cards, dominos, checkers or chess. But by far, the big event of the evening became a contest of darts. A large Australian with a booming voice was taking on all comers.

"I can beat him," she announced as she finished her third beer.

"I know you can," he said and was about to explain why she shouldn't, but she was too quick. He ordered another beer and watched her approach and issue the challenge. The cold brew went down as smoothly as the first two matches. Dallas was able to hold her own against the big Aussie but could not put him away. Tadda bought two more beers and walked one over to Dallas. As he walked away he saw trouble brewing in the big man's eyes. In an effort to improve her aim and mobility she had tied her shirttail tightly above her waist, exposing the smooth tanned skin of her midriff. The visual effect was stunning but, as Tadda feared, the big man misunderstood her intentions. The Aussie reached over and wrapped his fat fingers around her bare waist. As he saw the stranger touch his lover, Tadda became enraged and quickly moved back toward them. Dallas saw him coming to intervene and knew there was no need. She could handle this herself: in many ways she was more capable than he of dealing with this Neanderthal. Dallas unceremoniously removed his hand, glared into his eyes, and without looking threw her last dart into the wall way wide of the target. "You win," she growled and moved to intercept her lover. She pressed her body as close to him as she could, wrapped one of her long legs around his, and kissed him hard. "Come on, darlin', we have better things to do." The big man had won and lost in one fair stroke. He tried to block their exit but his friends corralled him back to the bar.

The couple kissed once, twice, and again as they rushed back to the boat. An aromatic haze lingered about the docks as the smoke from a dozen charcoal fires mingled over their heads, but the lovers were oblivious. The thin line that separates love, hate, and rage had been blurred by the beer and broken by her behavior. They barely made it into *Donwanna*.

The cabin proved to be too hot. They dressed and return topside for the last beer of the evening. They held each other quietly as they drank. She smiled at him, rose, and walked forward. *War Eagle* would arrive tomorrow and Steamer would take her lover from her. A slight gust of wind caught her by surprise.

"Out of the northwest," Tadda said as he walked up behind her and encircled her waist with his arms. "Wind's a-changin'." She shivered, took his hand, and led him below.

12

With a thunderous crack, a white-hot bolt of lightning split the ink black sky. Captain Steamer Causey closed his eyes tightly in a vain attempt to preserve his night vision.

"What's going on, Steamer?" Jackie was visibly shaken as another wave sent the boat careening into the trough.

"Don't worry about it," Tadda said as he bit into a sardine and mayonnaise sandwich. "Just a blow, means we're in for a long night, eh Cappy?"

"You said it, Tadda. Jackie, if we were further south they'd call this a 'brave west wind,' a little further north it'd be a tropical disturbance. Hell, the weather guy on the TV in Miami'd just say it's an interesting cloud formation, but don't worry, he's keeping his eyes on it for us."

"One thin' 'bout da tropics, you git ya weather reports at least three hours before all dem trustin' souls dat listen to the radio," Tadda said as he braced himself against the chart table.

"Up close and personal, just like they say in the travel guides...." Steamer was never able to finish this thought, because another bolt instantly filled the night sky like the serpentine forked tongue of the venomous cobra. The rusty steel hull lumbered up yet another wave, tipped awkwardly to starboard, then slid broadside in a seemingly endless freefall, crashing into the sea at the foot of the mammoth wave. Somewhere lost within the din of the howling wind and the pounding sea, a snap and a metallic ring signaled the destruction of the sea-chest induction pipe and the inevitable end of the *Donwanna*.

"Something's wrong, Tadda, she's not recovering!" Steamer shouted as he fought the wheel in an effort to steady the boat's motion.

"I'll take a look, Cappy," Tadda said over his shoulder as he hurried below. Another wave began to lift the boat but the quickly increasing weight squelched the motion and the fickle wave broke across her stern with all the vengeance of a spurned suitor. Suddenly there was silence. Death came to the *Donwanna* as easily and as instantaneously as it had to Tadda who had gone below in a futile attempt to stop the flooding. No engine, no lights, no radio, without steerage way the foundering vessel quickly fell broadside to the relentless swells. Steamer groped about in the dark wheelhouse for a flashlight. The next unexpected wave knocked him to the deck. The motion of the boat could no longer be anticipated.

Steamer found Jackie clinging to the handrail frozen with fear. He took her hand and led her toward the companionway that led below. He could smell the end long before he saw the stairwell. The warm sickening odor of fresh sea water greeted him as he opened the doorway. Three steps down and he was waist deep.

"Tadda! Tadda!" he called over and over. There was no answer but that of the storm which called out to him, *"You're mine, come out or perish!"*

The rising water backed them up to the wheelhouse. Steamer crawled to the leeward doorway, pried open the dogs and pulled Jackie and himself outside into the turmoil, into the power of the storm, into the hands of their God.

Hand over hand, they pulled their way aft. By the time they had reached the stack, the boat lay heeled over at forty-five degrees or better. Bracing his feet against the still warm steel Steamer pulled himself to windward and grabbed hold of the white canister that contained the inflatable life raft. Steamer held his breath as an angry wave broke over the side and crashed down upon him. As the water subsided he reached for his knife and began cutting the tethers that held the canister to its base. The stack now lay flat just above the surface of the sea. Steamer cut the final strap and slid the white fiberglass case onto the side of the stack. With a loud hiss the canister opened and the raft began to fill with air. Life asks no greater act of courage than it does of a man who must leave a sinking vessel. Steamer looked down—the last time the raft had been inspected was ten years ago. He closed his eyes and pushed Jackie into the raft, then rolled at the last minute into the partially filled inflatable, into the ultimate sailor's nightmare.

As the pressurized air filled the circular tubes of the raft, the aged surface rubber began to crack, peel and blister. Thin raw membranes stretched beyond their intended limits and powdery patches of orange rubber separated and fell like some form of vulcanized leprosy.

There beneath the smothering cloak of darkness, surrounded by the din and roar of an angry sea, lay two pitiable and insignificant souls. A momentary flash of lightning illuminated their situation. Jackie cried out but her words were consumed by the roaring wind, the relentless rain, and the rolling thunder. Steamer tried to stand. The sheer arrogance angered Poseidon and with a fist full of lightning bolts and a mighty breath the ancient god of the sea whipped the waters about the raft into a higher frenzy, hurling the pathetic human back into submission and slamming him against the walls of his rubberized tomb.

Steamer's head bounced off of the fully inflated upper chamber causing a ringing in his ears and the beginnings of the drums. The instability of the raft and the undulating swells that raced beneath them impelled their bodies together. Frightened and trembling, Jackie took hold of him, buried her face in his chest and held fast. He could feel the entire length of her now, her cool, wet flesh pressing against him with every roll. The drums in his ears grew louder and were joined by the chants of the hunters. She held on, shaking. He began to caress her head, running his fingers through her wet, matted auburn hair. She looked up into his face and spoke. But he heard nothing. The mighty gale that roared about them snatched the words from his ears. And the drums grew louder still.

The great cat pawed his way across the crusty land as the warm dry winds of the Serengeti brushed his coat. Steamer laid his head back he could taste the fresh blood of the kill in his mane. He was coming for her now. The hunters would not find him, could not stop him. He was coming to share with his lioness the power, the conquest, the conquering. Unannounced and unceremoniously the next wave forced the union. He wrapped his strong arms around her and held her tight. Gathering her supple, yielding body to his own. She looked up, her eyes wide, her mouth open. He kissed her long and passionately. In the dark of the night, in the height of the storm, without malice aforethought he took her as his own because she was his to take. She yielded because she had no choice. She yielded because it was her choice.

As the storm—and the drums—subsided, Steamer finally looked up and about. A small survival kit was lashed to the upper tube. The faded paint and the rusted clasps offered little hope of its usefulness. An emergency strobe light should have activated but the batteries were long since expired. He cursed Tadda with a lump in his throat and continued to rummage through the moldy bag. He found only a first aid kit, a mirror, a fishing kit, a package of stale crackers, and three bottles of water.

Morning broke tepid and sticky. It was as if the storm had sucked all the oxygen and left behind silent motionless doldrums on an infinite sea. Jackie laid her cheek against the chalked and flaking rubber. She looked over and saw Steamer relieving himself at the doorway. She too felt the need to go but when she realized the ridiculous positioning that she would have to do to accomplish that feat she decided that she would wait. In college, she had been known as "the camel" for her ability to control her bladder.

"Quick, get the bag! We have some fish under the raft," Steamer said. He took the bag from her and rummaged through it for a fishhook and some line.

Jackie fell back against the side of the raft. She was fatigued and queasy and felt like she weighed a thousand pounds. Steamer jerked about, hanging halfway out the door, then suddenly swung a small live Dorado fish into the raft.

"This'll do nicely," said Steamer. He was well into survival mode at this point and was worried about little else.

Jackie sat in wonder as Steamer went about the business of providing. The smell of the live flopping fish did not mingle well with the stifling air inside of the life raft. She was about to ask Steamer if she could move closer to the opening when he handed her a freshly sliced strip of flesh from the fish. She put it to her mouth and began nibbling on it.

"Just pop in your mouth and eat it quickly." Steamer said as he was cutting out the fish's eyes with his knife. "Did you know that the eyes of the fish contain enough drinkable water to keep a man alive?"

Jackie tried big bites and little bites: it didn't matter. The wad of raw fish she tried to ingest was unsustainable. It was as if she was getting no nutrients, just the never-ending taste of raw flesh and fish oils. And the smell, the nauseating smell, mingled with the smells of their own bodies and that of the rotting rubber raft. It quickly reached beyond her limits and she heaved. Retching in uncontrollable waves she threw herself about the raft. Before regaining control, her bladder gave way. As she lay there in her own filth, she finally broke down and for the first time in two days she wept.

Steamer instantly realized what he had done wrong. He had too quickly fallen back upon his training and failed to take time to bring her with him. Steamer re-moved his T-shirt, soaked it in the cleaner seawater beyond the door, and began gently and lovingly cleaning her up. He moved her so that her head lay quite near the door. Then he busied himself as best he could clearing the raft of her vomit. They could both smell the urine but he was too much a gentleman to mention it. Steamer reached into the supply bag and gave Jackie two crackers and a bottle of water.

Minutes became hours, hours became days. For the first few hours, Steamer regularly maneuvered to look out the door but there was nothing there but endless sea. Every time he moved toward the opening Jackie became more agitated. By noon he had given up and they both lay there motionless and silent.

Jackie awoke late in the afternoon as the merciless sun was waning. An ugly rash was growing along her legs and arms. She looked at Steamer's shirtless torso and saw that he too was suffering from sitting in the turbid salt water.

Suddenly there were voices and a rapping on the side of the raft. The two scrambled to the opening and beheld the greatest sight ever seen, a sailboat right there along-side their raft.

"Colin! Colin, there are people inside!" Polly cried out. "Can you get us closer?" With deft precision and a prac-ticed eye, Colin maneuvered *Fidelity* until she gently rode against the tattered raft.

Polly reached into the raft with the boat hook. "Here, grab hold and I'll pull you aboard."'

"Hold on! Polly, go get the boarding ladder," Colin said as he left the wheel and dove below. The two sailors helped Jackie, who was struggling up the rope ladder. Steamer's last action as he clung to the bottom rungs of the ladder was to take his knife and repeatedly stab the rubber raft section by section until the hissing of the escaping air subsided. Several minutes later they were seated in *Fidelity*'s cockpits. Polly brought them both some bottled water and tea cookies. Colin busied himself attempting to tie off the old raft so that they could tow it behind them.

"Don't bother," Steamer said, "it's not worth it, and besides, I never want to see that son of a bitch again."

"We can't just leave it here," Colin said.

"Just take your flare gun and dispatch it," Steamer said as he gulped down the last of the water. Colin reached down into the carefully organized lazarette and removed the kit containing the flare gun. At the last minute Colin had second thoughts about wasting flares. He went below then came back with a double-barreled sawed-off shotgun. He pushed the raft gently away from the sailboat, then fired. The double-aught shot tore large holes in the raft. Colin reloaded several times until the raft was completely sunk.

"You should give this a try," said Colin. "It's great fun."

"Have at it, friend. I am forever grateful that you picked us up."

Polly volunteered, "My name is Polly and this is Colin ... and we're on our way to Panama."

"I'm Jackie and this is Steamer. Our boat sank in the storm last night. Our friend Tadda is still on board," Jackie said with tears in her eyes.

Polly frowned in sympathy. "Jackie, you should come below and get cleaned up. I think I have some clothes that will fit you."

Jackie showered and washed her hair then stepped out into the stateroom. Polly had laid out on the bed and old faded pair of jeans, a brightly colored bikini top, and a white blouse. There was also a jar of lotion with a distinct coconut smell to it. She massaged some onto her arms and legs where the rash had ravaged her skin, dressed, and went top-side.

Jackie was having tea with Colin and Polly when Steamer emerged from the cabin wearing a blue Columbia fishing shirt and some lightweight cotton trousers.

"Come, get some tea, and tell us of your wonderful adventures on the high seas," Colin bellowed jovially.

Steamer was in no mood for this foolishness. But he could do little else.

"Not much to tell, really. The boat just sank from under us. I'm just so thankful that you came along."

"Steamer, would you like a little rum to stiffen up that tea?" Steamer readily accepted and the four slowly settled into what would be a long passage. It was a full two days sailing west by southwest when they found themselves slightly more than 20 miles off the Nicaraguan coast.

"We'll sail on another mile or two, then turn more southerly in order to skirt the Nicaraguan authorities," Colin said.

"We can't wait to get to Panama," Polly said. "We understand it is very easy to retire down there and we are so looking forward to it."

The words had barely left her lips when the boat appeared on the horizon. The old diesels moaned and groaned as the patrol boat race towards them. There was little doubt as to their intentions. The old patrol boat was rusty and unkempt with the word *Diego* scribbled alongside in spray paint. The crew was also intimidating. They wore filthy jungle fatigues with no insignias. They sported full beards and long hair that blew with the breeze. With total disregard for maritime conventions or the pristine nature of *Fidelity's* hull, they quickly came alongside.

"Where are you bound, *Señor*?" said the large man who appeared to be in charge.

"Panama. We should be arriving in about four days," said Colin.

"I will need to see your passports," the large man said as he stepped aboard *Fidelity* in muddy boots, while two other men armed with rifles kept close watch over the proceedings. Polly went below and in no time at all returned with their two passports and a large envelope with the boat's papers.

"Here is our documentation, but Jackie and Steamer are refugees from the storm, so I doubt that they have theirs with them."

The large man smiled, exposing a mouthful of crooked yellow teeth. "They will have to come with us then. Did you know that you are in Nicaraguan waters?" Two other crewmen unceremoniously escorted Jackie and Steamer aboard *Diego*. Colin wished with all his heart to argue the point. He knew exactly where he was and that he was well into international waters.

"I don't believe we are," said Colin, "but if it's true it was certainly unintentional and we will adjust course immediately."

"My friend, you are already in Nicaragua. Our entry fee here is two thousand."

"But we are not going to Nicaragua!" Colin said, and then decided it was pointless to argue. "Never mind. Polly, go get the man two thousand pesos."

"No. Dollars, my friend. Two thousand *dollars*."

"We don't have anywhere near that amount!" exclaimed Polly in shock and disbelief.

"So how much do you have?"

Colin reinserted himself between the hard man and Polly. "Three, maybe four hundred. The rest is in the bank and in Panama."

"I should confiscate this boat then, but I'm feeling generous today. I will take the four hundred dollars and let you go about your business." The transaction completed, the big man stepped back aboard *Diego*.

"You will take care of our friends, won't you?" Polly blurted out at the last moment.

The big man smiled again very broadly. "Yes, yes, we will take excellent care of your friends." He slapped his big hand twice on the cabin top and they all drove away with laughter and jeers.

Once underway, the screaming 671 Detroit diesel engine resonated off of the steel bulkheads, making communication almost impossible. The old boat smelled of untended bilges and diesel exhaust. After what seemed like hours the vessel slowed as it approached port.

The big man returned to the cabin and said, "Welcome to Nicaragua, my friends." He walked over to Jackie and ran his fingers through her hair. "I think that you have many friends who would be willing to pay a grand ransom for your return."

"There is no one," said Jackie quietly.

"That is too bad for you, but we have other ways to be repaid for our trouble. How 'bout you, 'Mr. Fisherman,' is there anyone who will pay for you?"

When the big man turned his attention to Steamer, Jackie saw her chance. She leaped on the man's back and grabbed him by the throat. She was not strong enough to take him down but the diversion was all that Steamer needed. In the blink of an eye he had driven the man to the deck. He tried to scream in agony but his ribs had been broken and forced into his lung. Steamer looked at Jackie and shouted for her to get his gun but it was too late. Two armed men entered from the wheelhouse and leveled their weapons at Steamer.

"*Atarlos*, tie them!" Jackie and Steamer had their hands unceremoniously tied behind their backs, and they remained under armed guard until the boat docked.

13

The old military jeep jumped from pothole to pothole as they raced up the mountainous road. Steamer and Jackie struggled to keep their balance in the cramped back seat. The large plastic zip ties they were bound with cut into their wrists, and without the use of their hands, balancing in the back of the jeep was impossible. The oppressive jungle heat soaked into them, and their clothes became drenched in sweat. The one thing that bothered Steamer the most was that they had not been blindfolded. "I guess there's no need if they are only taking us one way," Steamer thought to himself as he sized up the situation.

There was one driver and two guards, one in front with a sidearm, and one sitting precariously on the back of the jeep. The one in the back could be easily discharged and the driver's weapon was holstered. If only the one in the front seat could be distracted. But Number Two, as Steamer called him, was cold. His eyes were intense and menacing. The others seemed to answer to him and he never took his eyes off of his captives.

For two full hours they bounced down the remnants of the old road. Steamer looked up and saw the hacienda estate with the large white walls that stood like a fortress atop the mountain. This would be his only chance. Steamer looked back and calculated the distance to the rear guard. He stopped fighting the motion of the jeep, planted his feet solidly on the floor, and using the momentum of the vehicle he thrust his head back. The action took the guard completely by surprise. The impact caught him squarely in the face and blood spewed from his broken nose. The last sound the rear guard heard was the harmless discharge of his shotgun as he tumbled head first onto the rocky road. With all the speed he could muster, Steamer twisted his foot around to attack Number Two but he was not quick enough. Number Two grabbed Jackie by her hair and pressed his pistol to her head.

"Sit down, or she dies!" Steamer locked eyes with his opponent and knew that they were done. He sat back slowly in complete resignation.

The driver slammed on the brakes. Number Two swung the pistol around and took aim at the driver.

"*Conduce!!* Drive, damn you!"

"But, my brother, we must go back!"

"*Está muerto.*" Number Two said, "As you will be if you do not do as I say!"

The driver turned forward, his face showing the fear and the loss that had been wrought upon him. In silence the group continued on.

Guards at the gate waved them through and Steamer could see many more placed along the wall. The couple was unceremoniously drug from the jeep and pushed through the front door of the palatial house. An aide led them directly to General Santiago's office.

"My General," Number Two said, "these two tried to sneak into our country. On the patrol boat, they tried to kill Miguel. I believe this woman is the sister of the whore you sold to *La Gallina Roja*." Number Two drew Steamer's knife that he had confiscated earlier and pushed Jackie hard against the wall. They were other people in the room but Steamer concentrated on the menace that now faced him directly.

"This one, too, should bring us a good price. Here, I'll show you." With the knife at Steamer's throat, number two deftly unbuttoned Jackie's blouse. She quivered as the sweat that covered her body quickly cooled newly exposed skin. Sweat beaded up all around her face and dripped from her nose. Jackie's body shook with fear as Number Two turned his attention to her.

"See, General." Number Two slid the blade of the knife beneath her bikini top and cut it open. Her breasts undulated with the violence of the attack and the sudden exposure. Jackie turned her head in shame and let go the fearful cry she had been stifling.

"Four inches," Steamer said to himself. "Just get that knife four inches away from her and I'll make you eat it."

"Leave her alone!" Steamer shouted. The diversion worked. Number Two stepped back and turned but he never saw Steamer's foot. The perfectly aimed kick impacted the guard's elbow, careening the razor sharp edge of the knife across his face and severing most of his ear.

The victory was short-lived. Steamer slumped to his knees as the air left his lungs. Another guard had caught him squarely in the back with the butt of an AK-47 rifle.

Through all the pain and confusion, Steamer thought he heard a familiar voice. He looked up and through blurred eyes he saw Maxwell. The big man was walking toward him clearly agitated and flailing his arms wildly about.

"God damn it, Santiago! What the hell kind of Mickey Mouse bullshit is this? My associate over there is holding a duffle bag containing three million dollars. A down payment on the largest arms deal you and I have ever pulled off. And your goons over there bring in a couple of tourists to rough up for exactly what I don't know. Hell, General! If I didn't know better I'd swear you were trying to fuck this one up again!"

The general stood and tried to get in a word of apology.

"I think this has all gone to shit. 'Code Brown,' we like to call it. General Santiago, you've got three minutes." Maxwell was now speaking directly into his watch.

Commander Thomas Green with Seal Team Four hovered in one of four Black Hawk helicopters just above the tree line on the downwind side of the complex.

"That's the signal. Let's get them out of there."

Santiago walked toward Maxwell, turning his back on Tony, the second member of the CIA team. That was his last mistake. Three rapid shots from the Beretta and half the general's head was gone. Maxwell drew his and in seconds the room was secured, all but for one guard who now knelt, wept, and pleaded for his life.

"No such luck, Pedro." With cold steel eyes, Maxwell fired once, killing the man instantly.

From outside, the sounds of helicopters and small arms fire could now be heard.

"Okay, they're here," Maxwell said as he cut the zip tie on Steamer and returned his knife. "Let's get the hell out of here."

Steamer freed Jackie who quickly arranged her clothes as best she could. Steamer wrapped his arm around her and followed Maxwell and company to the back door. At the door they were met by two large men dressed in full high-tech battle armor. Maxwell ordered the men to get the girl to the chopper.

"Just a minute, Hoss." Maxwell put his hand out and stopped Steamer. "I've got a mission for ya. That girl's sister is still alive. These assholes sold her to a whorehouse down in Managua. I've got a plan for you to save her and make us both rich at the same time. When we get to the helo, hit me hard and take the duffle bag. I'll make sure you get away. Work your way down to Managua, buy the girl, then buy your way home. Nobody but me knows you were ever here. I'll report the money missing on a blown mission. You and I can divvy it up later."

Steamer was taken by surprise and unsure of how to answer. "How will I find you? And what about Jackie?"

"You got it wrong, Bubba. I'll find you. The girl will be fine." With that, Maxwell spun hard to his right and dropped the bag.

"The son of a bitch hit me!" he said as he climbed into the Black Hawk. "Leave him, let's get out of here."

The choppers rose high in the air, carrying with them the noise and confusion of combat, and Jackie. With all his heart, he wanted her to stay with him, but he knew she would be safer in the hands of the American military. Reluctant as he was, he had been handed a job to do first, and would have to worry about her later.

Steamer was alone in the silence of the dead. His mind went instantly back to the jungles of Southeast Asia. He crouched low, looking for "Charley" behind every tree. He stepped silently and all of his senses were on high alert.

How he got here no longer mattered. He had a mission and how it was to be executed was all that mattered.

He looked about the dead bodies that lay where they fell, until he found one about his size. Dressed as a guerrilla he could travel armed because he had no intention of being unarmed in this hellhole again. The fatigue shirt was wet and sticky with blood and he thought he might use this to his advantage. In addition to the uniform he collected two 9mm pistols with five magazines, and an AK-47 with three magazines.

He tossed the duffle bag in the back of the jeep, put the rifle in the passenger seat at the ready, pulled the hat down over his eyes and started down the road.

He had traveled less than a half hour when he met an oncoming jeep. He pulled over to the side of the road and placed the rifle across his lap.

"*Adónde vas?*" the driver yelled as they came to a stop beside him.

Steamer spoke Spanish but not well enough to pull this off. He showed them his bloody shirt, doubled over and mumbled "hospital."

The three men exited the jeep and hurried to their wounded *compañero*. As they approached the jeep, the Kalashnikov rifle came to life spitting fire, smoke, and lead on full automatic. In seconds, Steamer was again alone.

The road continued toward the coast. He passed a bus and an old pickup. The inhabitants waved but didn't stop.

Steamer arrived at Puerto Cabezas by midday. The uniform of the dead man reeked of perspiration, human blood, and fear. He abandoned the jeep on a roadside by the market.

"I can't explain this," he said to himself as he removed the shirt. He swung the duffle bag over his shoulder and walked slowly through the market. At his first opportunity he bought a tacky tourist shirt and strolled through the line of shelters that sold everything from bread to fresh fish.

"*Cuanto*, how much?" he asked as he picked up a bottle of water and some savory cheese. He paid for his lunch and continued on down the street and around the corner, and then he saw it. An old Mercedes was parked outside a shop with a sign in the window "*En Venta*." He entered the store.

"*Cuánto para el coche*, how much for the car?" Steamer asked. The storeowner was German and spoke perfect English.

"I am asking one thousand dollars or the equivalent."

"I'll take it," he said, and counted out ten one hundred bills. In less than twenty minutes Steamer threw the duffle bag into the trunk slid behind the wheel and for the first time in days he relaxed.

The ride inland to Managua took well into the night. He found a hotel and got his first shower in days. With a towel wrapped around his waist, he lay on the bed and formulated a plan, then drifted off to sleep.

As he checked out of the hotel, he asked the clerk about the adult entertainment scene in Managua. The clerk gladly shared what he knew.

"*Gracias*," Steamer said, then loaded the Mercedes and drove toward Managua.

The pace and the traffic accelerated as he approached the capital city. The hustle and bustle gave him additional cover. He was no more than a face in the crowd by the time he arrived at the Hilton Princess Managua. A hundreddollar bill covered the need for his privacy. He checked into a suite as "Steven Reid." The Hilton was almost a self-contained city catering to the well-to-do. He spent the day shopping and grooming. A haircut, some nice clothes, and a massage. He waxed his moustache, slicked back his hair and became Steven Reid, the foreman of the lead team of an oil company.

Steamer's first stop was at the Banco Central de Nicaragua. The bank president was again German and spoke fluent English.

"So, Herr Reid, you wish for two numbered accounts containing one million American dollars each, a ten thousand dollar operational account with a credit card and a safety deposit box. Is there anything else I can do for you?"

"No, I think that is about all," Steamer said as he stood and offered his hand. It was strange how a large amount of cash bypassed the need for identification and regulations.

He returned to the hotel and went to the restaurant for lunch. As he ate, he talked with his waiter.

"*Habla usted Inglés?*" Steamer asked.

"*Si, un poco,*" the waiter replied.

"Do you know of *La Gallina Roja*, The Red Hen?"

"*Oh, si!*" The waiter perked up.

"How do I do business there?"

"I will arrange a cab for you this evening."

"Thank you, my friend," he said as he gave the waiter a hundred dollar tip. "I would like the service to be first class. Do you understand?"

"*Si Señor, y gracias mi amigo.*" Steamer signed for the meal, stood, and walked to his suite. He spent the afternoon availing himself of the amenities of the Hilton. At supper he was served by the same waiter who verified that Señor Reid would be paying cash for the car.

"I believe you will be happy, *Señor.*"

"Thank you, Emilio," Steamer said as he passed him another hundred. Emilio accompanied Steamer to the front entrance and pointed to a limousine. Steamer sat alone in the back and held his newly purchased briefcase. The ride took twenty minutes then they turned into a well-manicured villa on the outskirts of town. Steamer was escorted into the office just inside the entrance and to the right.

"Señor Reid, so very good to meet you! I am Geraldo Jardinero. Please come in and sit down. May I get you a drink?"

"That would be nice. Scotch, unblended, neat."

"Of course." Geraldo said and picked up his phone. "Whatever you want is yours."

'You received an American woman some months ago from General Santiago."

"*Si.*"

"I wish to buy her from you."

"Do you mean for the night or the week?"

"No, I wish to purchase her from you."

Geraldo's demeanor changed. "My friend, that would be very foolish of me."

"I am prepared to offer you one hundred thousand pesos."

"No, I could not consider less than two hundred thousand American dollars."

Steamer took the briefcase and placed it on Geraldo's desk. He opened it, made sure Geraldo saw the Glock that Steamer then removed and placed in his waistband.

"There is two hundred and fifty thousand dollars there. Please bring her to me."

Geraldo wanted to ask more questions but the money stared at him and said more than he needed to know. He quickly closed the briefcase and again picked up his phone. Within minutes Brenda was brought to him. Her resemblance to Jackie was unmistakable. She was dressed in high heels and a party dress, but drugs and her captivity had taken its toll; her eyes were lifeless and she stumbled. Steamer thanked him and escorted Brenda to the limo.

Safely inside and on the way, Steamer started the explanation.

"Brenda, Jackie sent me to get you."

She looked scared and confused and put her hand on Steamer's thigh.

"No," he said calmly, "you don't have to do this anymore. You are free. I'm going to take you home." They returned to the hotel and sat and talked and he told her the whole story of how he came to find her. They went to sleep and every few hours throughout the night Steamer heard Brenda take a shower.

Morning broke, Steamer ordered breakfast in the room. He and Brenda went to the shops that surrounded the lobby. They bought her some basic outfits, toiletries, and makeup. Steamer bought a pay-as-you-go cell phone, a computer, and a phone card. Brenda slipped into withdrawal symptoms so they returned to the room. Steamer called the desk for and ordered some aspirin, vitamins, and Gatorade for her. He turned to tell her but she was once again in the shower.

He used the cell phone to call Jackie, who was very relieved to hear from him, and told her everything.

"We are going to the embassy in the morning, tell them we were robbed, and try to get new passports. See if you can buy us plane tickets for Sunday and send them to my email account. We are going to change hotels and go back to our real names."

The next few days proceeded as planned, but slowly. All the while, Brenda got stronger and stronger.

"It was horrible," she said quietly one morning at breakfast. Steamer put down his fork and reached for her hand. She pulled away and closed her eyes tightly in a vain attempt to keep the nightmare from returning.

"This was to be the honeymoon we never had. On the day that we arrived, the charter service did not have our boat ready so they traded us for a nicer boat that was scheduled to leave the next day. We were so excited and toasted our good fortune. We didn't know, how could we have known that General Santiago had chartered that boat." There was a long pause as Brenda steadied herself and took a sip of her juice.

"They came on us while we were sleeping. We were wearing only nightclothes," her voice broke as she began to cry. "We had no chance, none at all. They drug us out on deck and were screaming at us in Spanish. Neither Wayne nor I understood a word. They tore the boat apart obviously looking for something." There was a long pause, and her lip began to quiver. "Then one of the soldiers started groping me and Wayne came to my defense." She looked deep into Steamer's eyes with a longing he had never before seen or experienced. "They shot him, just like that. One second my love was there by my side and the next second he was gone. They pushed his body overboard and all that was left of my precious Wayne was the blood pooled in the cockpit."

No one spoke after that. They both ate in silence: there was nothing further to say. Her life had changed in an instant. Everything and everyone that she loved had been ripped from her and she was now the prisoner of ruthless men.

By Saturday he could hear her singing in the shower. By Sunday all was in order and they boarded a plane for Bimini.

14

The four-hour trip to Fort Lauderdale on *War Eagle* was slow and uneventful. Steamer was in no hurry to return to the mainland. There was nothing for him there and he knew it. Suddenly, a sailfish free-jumped to the south. Finely honed instincts took over and Steamer wanted to give chase, but quickly remembered it was not to be on this trip.

War Eagle strained against her moorings at Marina Del Mar, ready to be done with this mess. True to his word, Maxwell had found them. The sisters sat below side-by-side in the main salon, holding hands and consoling each other. They had been forever scarred by the unchecked events of the world and by man's inhumanity.

As he descended the ladder he paused momentarily to watch a school of tarpon glide beneath the pier. He thought about the thrill of doing battle with one of these giants. No matter, like so many things in his life, this trip had been beyond his control.

"We'll be in Fort Lauderdale for another day or two," he said as he approached Maxwell. The big man was seated in the fighting chair as if it were a throne. He cupped his hands and lit another of his Cuban cigars.

"One of the many perks of this job." He took a long draw then slowly exhaled. "And certainly one of the finest."

"I haven't been back to the mainland in a good while," Steamer's voice was full of hesitation as he spoke. "I hope there won't be any problems with Customs?"

"Problems? Son, I specialize in problems!" Maxwell reached into his gym bag and handed Steamer a long brown envelope. "Don't you remember? You've already been cleared for this trip," he said flatly, "and your work visa has been extended another three years. The documentation's all there. Now, I believe you have an envelope for me."

Steamer reached into his back pocket. His hands were shaking as he handed Maxwell the money. "It cost me more to get her out than we expected."

"That's okay, son. It's all funny money anyway."

"I know. Well, it's all there just like you wanted; ten thousand in cash and the rest deposited in an offshore bank. It has all been arranged exactly as you ordered." Steamer's voice was glum.

"Cheer up son, ya got a million dollars for ya trouble, nobody got hurt, and good old Uncle Sam don't know a thing about it. I like it when a good plan comes together! I'll stay in touch, boy. I'll have another job for you soon."

"No. I'm done. I want nothing more to do with you or your agency."

Maxwell just smiled. "Don't be stupid, boy. You've stolen three million dollars from the United States government. I own you! You got one choice and one choice only. Do as I say or spend the rest of your life in Leavenworth. *Comprender?*"

The graying sky and the fresh north wind sounded the alarm of the approaching front. The dark brown waters of the American coast felt alien to Steamer. Government agents dressed in suits and dark glasses lined the dock at his assigned berth.

With cold precision and unfeeling efficiency the sisters were escorted from the yacht and processed back into the country. Maxwell and his companions slowly walked away and vanished into the crowd that had begun to gather near the fuel dock. Steamer became painfully aware of his position as hired hand and began to wash down the boat. Just for a second he looked up. Jackie stood on the dock, her silent tears crying out to him for comfort. A surge of emotion welled up within him. He wanted to run to her and hold her in his arms. But their worlds had turned once again. The knot within his stomach held his feelings in check. There was so much to say; yet he said nothing. In silence and pain he turned away.

When he looked again they were all gone, all but one lone vision of despair. Dallas stood near the end of the dock staring into the murky depths, the last vestige of inconsolable hope. She had come to confront him, wearing a red satin dress that accentuated her Latin beauty. Steamer climbed onto the dock and walked toward her. He felt cold and lost, but at least he knew he could do this one good thing.

"Dallas," he said as he approached near enough to inhale her intoxicating perfume. The handkerchief she held against her face was no longer necessary for she had cried beyond tears. She lowered the cloth; her makeup was impeccable.

"I promised Tadda that I would take care of you if anything were to happen." Steamer's words cut through her like an arctic wind. "I want you to have this." He handed her an envelope filled with money. "Tadda would want you to have it."

"You have no right to even speak the name of my lover," she spat. She opened the envelope, removed the bills and flung them to the ground. "*Tu perro*, you dog, I will not take your Judas money. Let the blood of my beloved rot your soul forever!" Steamer dropped to his knees to retrieve the money. She turned in front of him and walked off, her shiny black high heels clicking as she turned, walked off the dock, and got into a waiting cab and went back to her life. Steamer never looked up.

Groveling on his knees about the dock, he picked up the bills one by one. This was all wrong. Had this become his life, prostrating and cowering before the likes of Maxwell? No, he would not become this man's puppet. He wadded up the bills, marched to the parking lot where Maxwell was getting ready to leave, and stuffed them into his hand.

"She's right, you know. It is blood money. It's cursed money and I'm done with it and with you."

With surprising quickness Maxwell reached out, grabbed Steamer's collar and pulled him close. "Be careful, boy. Bad things happen to stupid people. I'll be seeing you again because this isn't over, boy." Maxwell released him, slid the money inside his coat pocket, turned aside to talk with one of his minions, and disappeared into the car.

Steamer walked smartly to the boat. He knew what he had to do and he knew there was little time.

"Jimmy, take the night off. I've got to go see somebody."

"Thank you, Captain Steamer!" Jimmy said with a smile. "I'll see you back here in the morning."

Steamer never answered. He barely heard. He had a plan, but he had to act quickly. He scurried about cranking the engines and casting off lines. He'd climbed to the bridge and engaged the clutches when he saw Jackie coming up the ladder.

"What the hell are you doing here?"

"I don't know what you're doing but I know I need to be with you."

"This is dangerous. You should stay with your sister."

"Look, Steamer, I don't know how to say this. I don't know where you're going, but I have a strange feeling that you're really going to need me. Besides, I only feel safe and calm when I'm by your side."

He looked deep into her eyes. He wanted to argue with her, to make her stay safe, but he saw there was no convincing her. Besides, deep in his heart, he wanted her with him.

"Okay. Come on up and sit down."

"Where are we going?"

"We have to go see a man about a boat."

As soon as Steamer had cleared the jetties, he throttled up and took *War Eagle* to a full plane. He traveled due east until they could no longer see land, turned off all the electronics, then turned south.

"Why did you do that?" asked Jackie.

"They can trace us with land-based radar and GPS and God knows what else. I need a head start and I don't know what Maxwell is capable of. There's a guy in Key West that I think can help us," he said. "His name is Randy Harrison. He was with my Ranger unit. He and I have been in and out of more tight spots than you can imagine. When we left the Army, I got as far away from government service as I could. Randy stayed and worked around the edges. He has investments and contacts all over the world. If anybody can help us deal with Maxwell, he can. The last time I talked to him, he was in Key West. I believe he is our only chance."

"Do you really think Maxwell will come after you?"

"I'm as sure of that as I am of my own name. I am the only witness to what he has done and he's the type of man who believes you're either with him or against him. Trust me, he'll be coming."

"Can Randy help us hide?"

"I don't know what he can do but I know there's no other way and no other man I can trust."

The trip down the coast took the better part of six hours. Steamer idled into Key West Bight Marina.

"It's not safe to stay on the boat. There's a small guest-house just around the corner."

They secured the lines, bought some food at the Waterfront Market, then quietly walked the few blocks to the house. All about them were the sounds and smells of drunken tourists and revelers, oblivious to their plight. They walked past a homeless man sitting on the side of the road. Steamer thought to use him as a lookout but decided that the man was too far beyond usefulness. Five minutes later, Mr. and Mrs. Jones checked into the Poinciana House.

Marco was tending bar at Turtle Kraals in the middle of the week in the middle of his life. He had been there for what now seemed like an eternity. The same faces staring back at him, the same questions, the same drinks. Only the tide of tourists or the occasional "snotty yachties" who drifted in and out of Turtle Kraals provided diversion. At the end of the bar, Nick was talking politics with two commercial fishermen. Just outside the door, Marco could see the beginnings of a drug deal going down. He turned away. Suddenly, he was aware of two new patrons at the bar. He walked over and was in the process of asking what they wanted when he recognized Steamer.

"Steamer! Where in the world have you been? It's been what, three or four years since you've been here? Are you still driving *War Eagle*?"

"Yes, I am. She's tied up just down the dock. I've been real busy in the Bahamas. This is Jackie. Jackie, say 'hi' to Marco."

Jackie reached out her hand and said, "How are you, Marco?"

Marco responded, "What's a nice girl like you doing with a crusty old goat like this?"

Steamer cut into the banter before Jackie could answer. "Marco, I need to see Randy. Is he around?"

"You mean the 'mayor of Key West?'" He's probably holding court down at Schooner's." He meant the Schooner Wharf Bar. "I've heard he's been filling in for the captain on the Dry Tortugas ferry. He should be in here around five-thirty tomorrow."

"Marco, we're staying over at Poinciana House," Steamer said as he passed Marco a card. If anybody starts asking questions about me, how 'bout giving me a head's up? And, by the way, you still haven't seen me."

"Steamer who?" Marco said, as he put the card in his pocket. "I'll be happy to be your lookout. Now, what are you drinking?"

Steamer and Jackie stayed for a cocktail or two and then walked down the street in the still and muggy night air on what could be the last quiet night of their life. The sunset was warm and soft, and silent. On the way back to the guesthouse, they stopped and bought clothes for Jackie. Later, he sat nursing a bottle of beer and making notes on a scrap of paper. She was in the living room, deep into a book of Mayan secrets she had found on a shelf. *War Eagle* lay snug in her berth at the Cay West Bight Marina. Small brightly colored tropical fish darted about her bottom exploring the newly arrived hull tied to the transient dock. A large ancient barracuda drifted about in the shadows and the sounds of distant dolphins resonated through the water.

Getting ready took longer than expected. It felt unnatural to Steamer to not dress for dinner, but if they were going downtown to eat they had to make an effort to blend in. So he pulled out a pastel polo shirt, cargo shorts, and flip-flops. Jackie donned a long, turquoise blue sundress she had purchased earlier, and sandals from a shop down the street called Kino's.

They were walking tall as they stepped through the gate and into the great American party that is Duval Street.

"This is great!" she said, as she folded herself around his arm. She had never been to Key West, and found it all so different. The air was moist and heavy and held the sounds and the tastes and the smells of the carnival that lay ahead. They were still several blocks away and the combination of music being played in so many different clubs combined and drifted above the city. The blending of the music came together creating the heartbeat of the lost city at land's end.

As they neared the corner of Duval Street at Greene Street, they saw two men. One wore a black mustache, and both had a military posture. The one without the mustache held an expensive camera and was taking pictures of the crowd. Something didn't seem right.

Steamer and Jackie turned quickly into a tacky t-shirt shop.

"I don't know if they're two of Maxwell's men," he said, "but I don't want to take the chance. Let's wait until they move on." She readily agreed. They watched the men from near the door.

After a few minutes, a big crowd of revelers passed the shop. They walked out into the middle of them and passed by the two men unnoticed. As the crowd went by Captain Tony's Bar on the way back to their cruise ship, Jackie and Steamer ducked inside.

They looked around and he smiled at the look on her face. They had entered an eddy, a quiet inviting place with dull yellow walls, old oaken bar stools, a long horse-shoe shaped bar and a man sitting in the corner with a guitar and a microphone. The patrons were scattered about the room, some talking, some listening, and some solemnly nursing their drinks. They ordered rum and found a small table near the back wall. Her hair glistened with sweat and perfume. He ran his fingers gently through her curls and kissed her neck.

"The guitar player is amazing," he said as the musician began to pick a delicate and intricate guitar introduction. As he played, he closed his eyes and swayed as the song lines took him to another place. Then he shifted his head and began singing a beautiful piece of his own about Costa Rica with a smooth and gentle voice reminiscent of Eric Clapton. Some drunk tourist yelled, "Play some more Jimmy Buffet!" The pain in the singer's eyes was apparent. He sighed, finished his song, took a long swig of beer and began "Margaritaville," but if you listened carefully, another song lay just below the surface. The manager gave him a thumb's up and the guitar player mentally flipped him off.

Steamer and Jackie sat close, touching arms and legs, hands and hearts. They ordered another drink and listened while the singer sang the most beautiful rendition of "Layla" they had ever heard. He put down his guitar, walked over to the bar and ordered a shot of Sambuca. Several people spoke to him and tried to tell him how much they enjoyed his music. He gave a well-practiced and polite answer but he remained firmly inside his shell.

They worked their way down the street to a place called the Front Porch Café. They entered the clean white clapboard house with a large second story porch overlooking the street. They took a table close to the edge where they could see the throngs of happy vacationers passing beneath them.

They drank two Coronas, *con lima,* and ordered conch fritters for an appetizer, then decided they should slow down. They had only one more beer with dinner. She had the yellowtail and he ordered fried grouper. He took her hand across the table and kissed her fingers. They finished with coffee and shared a piece of Key Lime pie.

From this vantage they could see the entire scope of the celebration. The two men were gone from their previous position at the corner. Beneath them moved a wave of humanity. Together the people formed a living quilt with colorful shirts and hats representing every club, college, country, and cause one could imagine. The gathering was of singular mind and purpose. They danced as one in the celebration of sunsets, and life, and of this one amazing moment in time that would never be again.

"Are we ready to go?"

"Absolutely," she said as she released his hand and stood up to leave.

They moved with the crowd as the celebration moved from bar to bar up and down Duval Street. They were in the midst of a tide of humanity, every age, size, race and creed. Together they became the lifeblood of the city flowing through the island. They walked on, past Sloppy Joe's, Fat Tuesday's, and The Bull and Whistle. They peeked in at the crowd at Margaritaville. They stopped for a drink at a place called the Hog's Breath Saloon. They sat and took it all in, the sights the sounds, the smells, the energy.

Steamer put his arm around her and said "Let's go." Outside the party was in full swing. They walked and talked for what seemed like hours. They finally found themselves down at Mallory Square. They walked to the water, on the edge of town, on the edge of the island, on the edge of the universe. A long mournful whistle sounded the departure of a tug and barge outbound in the narrow winding channel that lead seaward, away from this place of sanctuary. With a slow and lingering pace they made their way back to the guesthouse. Once they were safely inside, he lit the lamps, and checked that his weapon was still where he had hidden it. Time was suspended but never stopped.

The new moon waned and they slept as they never had before. Tomorrow they would face the new world but tonight they were safe and happy cocooned in the lost city at land's end.

They woke sweaty and stale. It was against every fiber of Steamer's makeup to wait this one out but he could do nothing. "So what's the plan?" asked Jackie.

"Just sit tight until we meet with Randy." Steamer kissed her and headed for the shower. They dressed leisurely and as was the nature of this city, and slowly set out into the tropical morning. The day dragged by, with no sign of anyone suspicious lurking about, and by mid-afternoon they made their way back to Turtle Kraals.

"Hey, Marco," Steamer said as he surveyed the bar then found a seat away from the door. It wouldn't happen like this. Not in a public bar. But at least he may be able to spot them coming.

"Rum and Coke?" Marco asked.

"Tall ones and make them light, please; it's still early," Steamer said. "Seen anybody new since yesterday?" Marco shook his head no and placed the drinks on the bar.

Steamer looked around. There was a commercial fisherman with a thick Maine accent standing by the door making a deal with a mechanic, and a group of three locals drinking at the other end. Suddenly one of the locals threw his drink on an old man.

"Fuckin' asshole!!!" The old man screeched.

"Nick, watch your mouth or you're gone."

"He threw his drink on me."

Marco's demeanor changed drastically. "I think the bunch of you have had enough. Everybody out, or I'll call the cops and ban you from here for life. It's your choice."

The three men grumbled and complained and staggered out the front door.

The rest of the afternoon went quietly. At about five-thirty Randy came busting through the door.

"Steamer, you old coot! Where the hell you been?"

"Looking for you, Randy," Steamer said. "I need your help. Sit down. I need to give you the long version."

The three talked quietly near the end of the bar as the sun dissolved slowly to the west.

"Shiiiit, you don't need help. You need a fuckin' miracle!" Randy said. He sat back and lit a cigar and thought for a minute. "Here's the keys to my boat. It's a piece-o-shit trawler. Take it out to the Marquesas and hide out until I get a hold of you. There's an AK-47 on board with enough ammo to hold off a small army for a month. Get in tight on the Northwest corner and you should be able to see anyone coming from there."

"How will you contact us?"

"Oh don't worry yourself 'bout that. I'll be real noisy

when I come because my goal is always not to be shot with my own gun."

Then as quickly as he had arrived, he was gone. Steamer and Jackie finished their drinks, paid the tab, then walked off to check out of the guesthouse and find Randy's boat.

Randy made two phone calls then hailed a cab to the airport. An hour later, in Miami, a government car swept him away.

"Rand-Eye! Good to see you again, boy! How you doin'?"

"Just fine, Maxwell, just fine," Randy said as they shook hands and went inside his office.

"Cuban?" Maxwell said as he offered Randy a cigar.

"Don't mind if I do. I got you a present," he said as he bent to light the cigar. "Seems like your rabbit ran down my hole." Randy took a deep puff and sat back into the big chair opposite Maxwell's desk.

"That so? What makes you think I've got a rabbit?"

"Is that how you want to play it? I come here in good faith to hand you a stooge on a silver platter and you turn me away?" Randy got up to leave.

"Sit down, Randy. Whatcha got in mind?"

Not much. You give me ten thousand dollars and I guarantee to have Steamer Causey and his girlfriend in a secluded place for you day after tomorrow."

"How 'bout a hundred grand to take care of this one for me?"

"No." Randy stood. "I'm done cleaning up after you. I'm staying at the Hilton. Deliver the money and I'll deliver your putz. And they'll be on my boat, so no blood, no bullets and no bombs. Take them out real clean, ya hear?"

Maxwell had no choice but to agree. Randy closed the door, left the building, and called a cab.

15

Great black clouds seethed and boiled all along the northern horizon. The western sky, filled with a fiery sunset, battled the impending storm for its rights to the sky. Lightning skipped and arced from cloud to cloud and the sharp report of thunder rolled towards them.

"We should go below soon. Wind's swinging around," he said from beneath his straw hat.

She looked up from her book at the gathering storm.

"Suppose you're right. Not enough light to read by now. Anything we need to do up here?

"Naw, button her up and ride it out. Doesn't look too bad."

She went straight to the shower and began her ritual. He secured the hatch, closing out the world, and lit the small hurricane lanterns that hung gimbaled to the bulkheads. By the time she had secured the water, the light fragrance of scented soap drifted about the intimate confines of their small cocoon.

She stepped from the shower, wiping the water from her face. Their hands met as a gust of wind buffeted the small boat causing it to heel slightly to starboard and disturbing her balance. He caught her and pulled her to him. She stood wrapped firmly within his arms. Wind-driven waves began to build and march in steady lines beneath the hull. The lovers kissed as the boat began a slow undulating roll. He gathered his hands around the back of her neck and kissed the moisture from her face. He held her close and inhaled her beauty. She smelled of shampoo and perfume, honey and raspberries, and all that was good on land or sea. She led him to the stateroom.

Around 2100, he got up, dressed, and said to Jackie, "I'll take the first watch and I'll need you to relieve me in a couple hours." She yawned and agreed and went back to sleep.

The storm continued its relentless advance. Its proximity increased its intensity. The howling wind interspersed with sharp reports of thunder and then the rain began, with big wet drops that splashed and splattered just overhead. The crescendo and syncopation continued until the rain became an unnatural deluge echoing and resounding round about them. Land, sea and sky battled for dominance and the conflict raged along the anchor line, sending vibrations of strain and concern along the gossamer thread which held them in place. The small boat lifted and pitched as the wind drove a large wave beneath them. The anchor regained its tentative hold and the bow steadied into the trough. The boat bucked and reeled with the fury of the storm. It was midnight before it passed over and moved on.

Jackie woke Steamer awoke around 0100. "Steamer, someone's coming!" He jumped out of the bunk and racked a loaded magazine into the AK-47.

No need. It was Randy. He pulled alongside in a disreputable-looking old lobster boat.

"Let's go! We've got work to do and not much time to do it," he said.

16

It was that time of morning, not quite light, no longer dark. The old fiberglass hull rode at anchor in harmony with the forces of nature. Ripples of gentle wavelets lapped along her sides. The anchor line stretched over the bow pulpit and reached down into the clear water. The heavy plow-shaped anchor dug in, holding fast to the white sand bottom. An ancient barracuda held station just below. Dark shadows circled just beyond detection.

Almost undetectable at first, the sounds began to change. The rhythm of the sea became unsettled as the plastic paddles made their way through the quiet water. There were muffled squeaks and groans, as the rubber dinghy rubbed alongside the boat's hull. Time passed in undisturbed silence. Suddenly there were two distinct noises: Maxwell and his hired killer climbed quietly over the side. Guns at the ready, they moved silently toward the cabin. Click. Maxwell's heart sank at the unmistakable sound of the trigger to the C4 arming itself. He knew instantly that Steamer and Jackie were no longer on the boat and that he had succumbed to his own trap. Maxwell thought of the many men he'd killed in the same manner. He knew that escape was impossible, and that the end was imminent. Damn.

The sky began to glow with a soft red hue towards the west. A brilliant white light appeared below deck. Instantaneously, the light filled the cabin, then spewed forth from every opening. The deafening crack of the explosion preceded the appearance of the flames. In seconds, the searing white light was transformed into a large golden fireball that engulfed the boat.

The explosion could be seen for miles. Even from an old lobster boat just beyond the reef some eight miles away.

"The deed is done, my friend," said Randy as he put down the glasses. "That poor fuck must have had a propane leak. And, by the way, all the evidence is destroyed. "Here," he said as he handed Steamer an envelope. "A going away present from Maxwell."

"You keep it. Put it toward a new boat. I have all I need," Steamer said as he remembered the location of the password to his Cayman Island bank account. "Now, take us back to Key West. I owe my lady one more shot at the Duval Crawl."

"Wait up, Sparky. I need you and your lady outta here pronto. In case you forgot I still have a mess to clean up."

Steamer and Jackie and their luggage were deposited back aboard *War Eagle.* They said their goodbyes and got underway for parts unknown. There was a cursory investigation. Randy had a prepared form that indicated that the boat had been stolen two days before. There was some concern at the CIA office in Miami. Certain codes were changed, files were shredded, and contacts were warned. But soon another government bureaucrat took his place and all that remained of Maxwell was consigned to a box in the station warehouse.

The remains of the burned out hull settled into the sand. Some noise was made about possible pollution and wreck removal, but a donation to the Conservancy quieted that down. Great barracuda stood guard over the wreck waiting, for any morsels to seep up from the sand. Wide-eyed divers began to poke around the formless hulk, hoping to find buried treasure.

EPILOGUE

It took some time for Jimmy to get used to Jackie being on the boat with them. He had said nothing when Steamer bought *War Eagle*. It was just one less level of management he had to concern himself with.

An investment group out of Miami bought the management rights to Shark Reef Cay. All the Bahamians got fine new red and white uniforms then went right back to business as usual. Steamer bought one of the large condominiums up on top of the bluff, but he and Jackie decided to remain on the boat.

At last all was quiet and at peace. One had to look hard to see the signs of the storm that had engulfed them. Now it was time to rest and prepare them for the adventures to come.

About the author

Captain Buddy Ward, the pen name of Leon B. Ward, III, is a native of Charleston, South Carolina, was graduated from The Citadel, and holds a master's degree from the University of South Carolina. After his graduation, he worked for Charleston County for almost a decade in the juvenile justice system, then became a tugboat captain working in Charleston Harbor for over thirty years. He is the author of *Tales of the Anna Karrue*, a novel about life aboard a tugboat, published in 1988 by Tradd Street Press. He has also written for *Power and Motor Yacht*, *Coastal Cruising*, *Latitudes and Attitudes*, and *Southern Boating*, as well as several other magazines, and for more than a decade was a staff writer for *The Water Log*, a local maritime journal. His collection of short stories, *Into the Mystic*, explores Charleston Harbor and the men who worked her; *Christmas Snapshots* collects his original Christmas stories; and *Together We'll Ride* relates stories surrounding horses and their riders.

More recently, Buddy and his wife Lee Anne have cruised aboard *Evening Star*, their beautiful forty-one-foot Islander Freeport sailboat, covering twenty-two hundred miles in almost five years and working at jobs around the waterfront along the way. Their adventure behind them, they are home again in Charleston, along with Skipper the golden retriever and Ellie the chocolate lab; and Captain Buddy has returned to writing about what he knows best.

Visit us at *www.qpbooks.com.*